STOLEN FROM MY BILLIONAIRE BOSS

A Best Friend's Brother, Age Gap Romance

JENNIFER RIVERS

This is a work of fiction. Names, characters, places and incidents either are the product of the author's imagination or are used fictitiously. Any resemblance to persons, living or dead, business establishments, events, or locales is entirely coincidental.

Stolen From My Billionaire Boss

Copyright © 2023 by Jennifer Rivers

All rights reserved.

No part of this book may be reproduced in any form or by any electronic or mechanical means, including information storage and retrieval systems, without written permission from the author, except for the use of brief quotations in a book review.

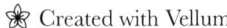 Created with Vellum

Introduction

All I want is to get my life started after college.

But when a string of gruesome murders sends my hometown into lockdown it's hard to find a place to live, never mind a job.

So I can't believe my luck when I land an interview at the flashy high-tech security firm.

Then I meet my new boss .... Damon Clark.

My best friend's older brother turned successful billionaire.

He's not the boy I remember.

His years as a marine have served him well.

His broad shoulders and chiseled arms have me clenching my thighs when I see how he looks at me with fire in his eyes.

But he's older and I am determined to keep things professional.

I agree to move in with him until I can find my own place but with our close quarters

and a tension between us that's undeniable, it's making it impossible to resist him.

Introduction

Now with the killer growing bolder, and a deadly threat that's been hiding in plain sight.

We're trapped in a dangerous game of cat and mouse.

All I wanted was to get my life started but now all I want is to stay alive......

Chapter One

ERIN

The entire town of Aubridge was on edge. For a place that had an "unlocked door" policy for every in-need neighbor since I was young, it was a stark contrast to the reality we were now in. Residents had rushed out to buy new security systems, new locks… dogs from the local pound. They were terrified and grasping at anything they could achieve some semblance of safety.

There had been a string of murders in the town. Two women, two different days, and nothing else in common… or nothing that the police were able to ascertain. From what I read in the newspaper, I found out that they were twenty-four and sixty-three. One was a widow, and the other a struggling artist. Both lived under the radar and didn't get out much. They were found in their homes… left splayed on the floor for anyone to find.

My parents had insisted on putting bars on my window, but I vehemently disagreed. As scared as I was, I was a firm believer in not living in fear. The killer only won that way. Besides, I felt a little safer knowing we had an ex-Navy SEAL living next door.

Damon was my best friend Cara's older brother. Their family had lived next door to mine for as long as I could remember. Damon purchased his parents' house from them when they wanted to downsize to keep it in the family. Cara and I were inseparable as kids, only being apart for the first time when I left for college.

Now I was back, and I needed to start my life.

"Erin! Get your butt down here! Your breakfast is gonna get cold!" my mom screamed from the kitchen.

She was a stickler for family breakfasts and was over the moon that I was back home. I tried to keep her excitement at bay by reminding her I planned to find my own place once the murders were solved. With my new master's degree in applied Behavior Analysis at the ripe age of twenty-six, I was ready to find a career that would play to my strengths. I needed to start my life.

"Coming!" I pulled my frizzy brown hair back into a tight ponytail and sprinted down the stairs.

Ellison was sitting at the table with my mom and dad, already chowing down. He hit a major growth spurt in high school, when he consumed everything in the house and never stopped. As the top security officer at Damon's company now, he'd probably needed it. He had sworn he would move out several times over the years, but he also didn't want to pay rent unless he absolutely had to, which was code for "I need a girlfriend first."

"Smells good, Mom. I need it today… gotta find a job." I popped a piece of potato into my mouth.

"Erin…" My dad set his fork down, ready to protest.

"Dad, please. I already know what you're going to say. And yes, I'll be careful. Especially after my big brother loaded me up with top-of-the-line self-defense tools," I laughed, holding up a pink pepper spray.

"That reminds me. Don't go advertising all of that. Keep it hidden… more effective that way," Ellison growled.

Will do, brother. He wasn't one for many words.

"Alright, thanks. Well, I had better get going." I lightly kissed my mom on the cheek and gave my dad a tight squeeze.

Ellison held his closed hand up for a fist bump as I walked off.

Before leaving, a quick change of clothes was in order. I needed something more professional, settling for my flowy rose-colored business tank and my black blazer. I grabbed my keys and sprinted out the door. I was jittery and excited, ready to start my job search. I was nervous, but the excitement at the prospect of being able to begin the rest of my life overpowered it.

I switched on the radio of my clunky but reliable 2007 faded-blue Jeep, and my fingers drummed on the steering wheel as I cruised down the road. Everyone was already out and about, off to their morning errands, jobs, and life.

I had the newspaper rolled up and placed firmly in my lap. Last night, I found a chance to browse the current job listings. There was an opening at the local elementary school for a guidance counselor, and another position for a "behavioral strategy advisor" at an unknown company. There was no name listed, only a number and an address. I had been able to schedule an interview at the Griffin Elementary School for this morning and planned to drive by the other address later.

As I pulled into the parking lot, I struggled to find parking. Cars were lined up, dropping off kid after kid, some parents walking their children to the front gate where they were met with the smiling faces of their teachers.

I returned a grin as I pushed past into the front office.

"Hi, I have an interview with the principal. I am Erin Summers." I handed my resume to the receptionist, who was less than pleased at my arrival. She seemed overwhelmed as she pushed a stack of papers to the side and silenced an incessantly ringing phone. She pointed wordlessly to an open chair, an invitation for me to sit.

Thanks.

I hummed quietly to myself, feet tapping on the floor. I was nervous. This was my first big job interview following my graduation. Books and test scores were one thing, but "people" had never been my thing. I always said the wrong thing or got too far in my head.

"He's ready for you, Miss Summers." The grumpy receptionist pointed towards the back of the office.

I thanked her as I passed by, taking a quick second to wipe my sweaty hands on my pants.

Here goes nothing.

"Come in," a strong voice boomed as I rapped on the door.

As I swung it open softly, I spotted a man in a large black chair who couldn't have been five years older than me, his dark hair neatly combed.

"Hello, Miss Summers, I'm Jordon Nash. Please, take a seat." He gestured to the chair opposite him.

"I'm happy to be here," I smiled, removing my jacket.

"We're happy to have you. To be honest, you'd be great for the position. Your level of education is quite higher than we usually require for a position like this. The higher-ups would probably smack me on the wrist for this, but you're *overqualified* for the job…" He trailed off.

His eyes wandered around the room, landing on mine.

He was keeping something from me, an unspoken truth hanging between us.

It was true. But the jobs I could obtain in this town were pretty dismal.

He fiddled with his hands nervously.

Oh shit, I'm not getting the job.

"I feel like I would be doing you a disservice by giving you the position." He spit out, his eyes cast down after he said it.

Shit.

"Please reconsider. I know that's a little bit bold saying as the applicant, but I know I would do an excellent job. Besides… isn't it my choice to decide if I'm too good for a job?"

I instantly regretted what I said as the words left my mouth.

The expression on his face changed from contrite to shocked and then landed on amused. He chuckled, relaxing significantly as he reclined back in his chair.

The corners of his lips curved into a boyish grin.

"That's fair, Miss Summers."

"Call me Erin, please."

"Okay… Erin. How about this? Look around a little bit. I know this town may not have *much* for someone with your degree, but if you still find yourself without employment, then we would be lucky to have you." He chuckled, handing me a business card.

Not the deal I wanted. But it's the card I'm being dealt.

"Absolutely. Thank you so much for your time, Mr. Nash." I stood, collecting my blazer and belongings.

"Please… call me Jordon." He held out his hand, grasping mine.

His handshake was firm… strong.

"Bye, Jordon."

I closed the door behind me.

Whew.

Disappointment coursed through my veins as I made my way back to the car. The receptionist didn't even feign a glance my way as I left. Maybe it was for the better. My mom was always a firm believer that "everything happens for a reason." She preached that a lot growing up. Perhaps the next job I would find would be the one for me.

My phone buzzed with a text from my mom.

Mom: Just checking in. How's the job search going?
Erin: Dismal. Will keep you updated.

My hands shook slightly as I input the address from the second job listing into the navigational system. I was definitely uneasy, but it wasn't as if I had any other option. I needed to find something… today. And I could trust my training to warn me if something was sketchy.

"Your destination is ten minutes away. Starting drive…" toned the GPS voice.

As I pulled in about ten minutes later, I admired the building in front of me—all sleek black with a gang of windows. The sign read "Security Operational Enterprise" in large bold lettering.

Pushing my way into the lobby, I marveled at the tech. There were electronic stands to check in and get clearance before you could move on to the elevators. The likelihood of me accidentally setting off one of the alarms was too high, so I opted for the live worker at the reception desk.

This woman was a lot friendlier than the grouch at the elementary school. She had a sleek blonde ponytail and a name tag that read *Cassandra*.

"Hi there, welcome to SOE. Do you have an appointment?" She eyed me carefully.

"I know this is a little untraditional, but I noticed a job listing in the paper. I wanted to come in and fill out an application… hand in a resume," I said, passing the paper to her.

"Fill this out, please." She handed me an employee intake application form and a pen, nodding to the reception area.

She picked up the phone and started talking at once. I couldn't hear what she was saying, but she was very animated as she spoke. I took the application to a table by the wall.

I filled out line after line of questions. It was the usual things. Name, date of birth, social security number… blood type? That was odd. I did my best to answer what I could, but some of the questions were a little invasive and bizarre.

As I handed the paper back to Cassandra, she asked me to sit back down and wait a few minutes. She was going to check the CEO's availability for a walk-in interview.

Great. Now I'm really nervous.

Meeting with a school principal was one thing… but the CEO of a rather impressive company was another.

Talk about intimidation.

"Yes, sir, Erin Summers," Cassandra said into the phone.

She hung up and called me back to the desk.

"You can go on up. Twelfth floor. He is expecting you." She returned my resume, sliding the copy she made into a newly minted folder.

I gulped, thanking her for her time as I passed the lobby to the row of elevators. There were four, which struck me as odd because there were only twelve floors.

The elevator whirred noisily up to the top floor. There was another desk as I walked in; this time, a young man sat at the helm.

"Miss Summers? Go in, door to your right. He's

expecting you," the young man commanded, barely glancing up from his work.

The big, frosted glass doors to my right eyed me intimidatingly.

Stop it. You're getting yourself worked up.

I knocked at the door, and a voice boomed from within the room.

"Come on in."

As I swung the door open wide, stepping in, I stopped dead in my tracks.

Him.

Chapter Two

DAMON

Her.

When the receptionist said her name, I stilled from shock. Of course, I knew she was back in town. It was a small town, so it was impossible not to hear every minute piece of news. Her arrival wasn't minute, though. She never went unnoticed… at least on my end.

Besides, she was right next door. Granted, I hadn't been home much in the last few days. Business had soared since the murders. Many of my guys had been designated to be on watch for those who could afford it. Of course, we also watched out for everyone else, free of charge. Almost all of my employees were born and raised here, and it was infuriating to see our friends and family terrified because of some sociopath. We were committed to keeping the town as safe as possible.

Ellison was one of my top guys, and he had let it slip

the week prior that Erin was finishing up with graduation and then packing up and heading home.

I always had a soft spot for her growing up. We were never anything romantic. She was much younger than me—close to fifteen years, and growing up, that would've been weird. It was an unspoken protectiveness I had for her. As my little sister's best friend and our neighbor forever, she was family. Not only that, but people in general tended to overlook her.

She was quiet, a little soft-spoken, and kept out of the cliquey circles.

"Come in…" I shuffled the papers around on my desk and cooled my exterior.

She was all hands as she jumbled the handle coming in. She was nervous, too… but not for the reasons I may have thought. When I saw her eyes widen with shock, I realized she hadn't expected me.

"Damon… I mean, Mr. Clark," she said as she shut the door behind her.

"Please, we're way past formalities. Sit down, Erin." I gestured to the armchair to the left of my seat.

She sat down, placing her belongings in her lap as she folded her hands together.

"I assume by your reaction that you didn't realize this was my company." A laugh emerged from my throat.

"Nope. I know that Ellison has mentioned the name before, but it completely slipped my mind."

"So tell me… why do you want a position with this company?"

"My education as an applied behavioral therapist major allows me different insight angles regarding behavior—what it means and how to respond. When I saw the listing for your position, I felt it would be something I would excel at. I scored at the top of my class, was valedictorian, and I pride myself on my ability to read someone within minutes of meeting them."

The confidence was evident. She was a pro at what she did. The confidence alone made me want to hire her on the spot. The fact that it was Erin… well, I don't think there was much she could have said otherwise to dissuade me.

"I'm impressed, Erin. To be fair, you have always been talented. Now, because I know you, and I want what's best for you, I have to ask, would you prefer working at a traditional facility as opposed to a security company?"

Her skills would be useful here. I don't want to feel like I'm cheating her out of a better opportunity, though.

"I'm sure. I know I could move somewhere else, gain employment at a larger company elsewhere. But I want to be here… This town—it's home. You won't regret hiring me."

"I know I won't. The job is yours if you really want it. I know you'll be an asset to our company." I stood, offering her my hand.

It felt weirdly formal, but formal was good for a job interview.

She stood, smoothing her shirt, and took my hand in hers. It felt… nice. Her hand was soft and her grip firm.

"So… when do I start, boss?" She laughed as she retracted her hand.

"It's Thursday. Take the rest of the week, enjoy your family. We can start fresh on Monday. That gives you a couple of days to change your mind," I joked.

Erin rolled her eyes in exasperation.

"I'll see you Monday." She started for the door.

"I look forward to it. The details for your first day will be sent to the email you left on file."

She gave me a quick nod before shutting the door

behind her. I exhaled and hadn't realized I had been holding my breath. Job interviews were never my forte, but it was fun this time around. Ellison never mentioned that she had been considering the job, but he likely didn't know. He was a stellar employee and a great friend. Otherwise, he kept his head pretty low to the ground and out of people's business.

A lot like his sister.

My cell phone started to ring. It was Cara.

"Hello, baby sister. What's going on?"

My niece Lila appeared on the video call. She had stickers pasted all over her face.

"Hi, Uncle Damon! Mommy and I were playing dress-up." She passed the phone to Cara, stood up, and did a twirl, showcasing her purple princess dress.

"You look beautiful, Miss Lila! What's Luke doing?"

The camera panned to Luke, crawling on the floor and trying to shove the pack of stickers in his mouth.

The phone fumbled, and I could hear Cara struggling to get them out of his hands.

Ah, the life of a parent.

"Sorry, Damon. These days, it's pretty much always a circus over here. I go back to school in about two weeks, too. I'm not sure how I'll manage," Cara sighed, her voice full of stress.

"I'm always here, you know that. You also have Jonas to help you. I know he works, too, but he's their father. He can help pick up the slack. It shouldn't always fall on you."

Jonas was a good dad, but my sister took the larger load when it came to caring for their kids, even when she did work. I didn't like it, but he was good to my sister… so I couldn't say much.

"You're right. I miss you. How's work been today?"

"You'll never guess who came into my office…"

"Who?"

"Erin," I confessed.

"I didn't know she was applying there. She didn't say anything. But that's great! She'll be a terrific addition, you know. I assume she got the job?"

"Of course she did. I have to get back to work, though. Bring the kids by for dinner soon?"

"Sure, Damon. Love you," she and Lila said in unison.

"I love you three." I hung up the phone, setting it back on my desk.

Rubbing between my temples, I realized it had been a while since I'd eaten anything. My breakfast for the morning consisted of a black coffee and half a banana. It was hardly a meal at all, but I had been running late, and well… I had an interview.

One that was more fun than I'd had at work in a while. It had been a lot more dismal than usual lately.

There was a sudden knock at the door. Half-expecting Erin, I yelled for the unknown visitor to come in.

It was my executive assistant, Charles. He had a stack of paperwork, which meant one thing only—we had an abundance of new cases.

"Looks like it's going to be a long day. Do me a favor. Can you order me some lunch, please? The usual."

"Certainly, sir." He handed me the papers and retreated.

As I leaned back in my desk chair and flipped through the cases, I found that it was more of the usual assignments. Lately, people were looking for extra safety around their homes or top-of-the-line security systems. Given that the victims had all been found in their homes, people were understandably worried about how well they could be protected within the four walls of their own homes. Our systems helped to alleviate some of that worry.

Police had released some information to the public, too. For one, they recommended never opening the door to anyone you don't know. They also advised traveling in pairs and only going out at night if necessary. They were not clear yet on where the murders were actually occurring—only that the bodies were found back in their homes.

People were reminded to be vigilant and stay aware.

Of course, this did not do much to lessen the public's fears. One by one, I called customers to set dates, ordered the systems online, and scheduled some of my employees to install them.

I looked up to a knock and Charles bringing in my lunch. It was already halfway through the work day, and I was wiped out. I almost always get a workout when I get home, but today, I wanted just to relax. It was the murders, and the extra hours of work because of them.

After lunch, I went on a few systems surveys and reviewed the installations. Ellison met me back at the office before he started his shift and brought a homemade apple cider donut with him, courtesy of his mother. Pastries were her specialty.

Finally, briefcase in hand, I waved goodbye to my employees as I headed to my car. Turning out of the parking lot, I cranked the volume on the stereo, singing along with *Blink 182*.

As I parked the car and walked up to the house, I took notice of Erin sitting on the porch, lost in a book completely. She hadn't looked up once, even when I locked the car.

I don't think I had ever noticed how stunningly beautiful she was until this very moment.

I shook my head at myself as I shut the door behind me. Appreciation… for a childhood acquaintance and new employee, that's all it was. Nothing more, nothing less. It couldn't be. Not only was it idiotic to express anything of the sort towards Erin, but I had to keep my focus on more important matters at hand, including the safety of this town.

The steaming hot shower helped me melt away the stress of the busy work day. As I wrapped a towel around myself and wandered into the bedroom, I immediately spotted Erin in her bedroom across from mine. Both windows had the blinds fully open. Her gaze met mine and shifted to the fluffy white towel wrapped around my waist. She looked back up and started to laugh as she raised her hand and offered a wave.

I returned the gesture and reached for the pull string on the blinds, slowly letting them fall.

I fell asleep with her smile on my mind.

Chapter Three

ERIN

The sound woke me from my sleep like a siren. My hands fumbled around the wall, searching for the light as I rubbed my eyes sleepily.

Boom.

There it was again. It sounded like it was right outside my window, something banging together.

I pulled on my robe and peered out the window. It was nearly pitch black, except for the slight glow of the street lights. I couldn't see much.

Sliding on my slippers, I shuffled down the stairs lightly, being careful not to wake anyone. I realized it was silly, because if the loud noise from outside didn't already do that, my descending down the stairs certainly wouldn't.

The odd sound had momentarily stopped, and the only noise that filled the house was my dad's snoring.

Sliding the flashlight from the kitchen in my robe pocket, I scanned the porch from the window once more before stepping out. Just as it had stopped, it started once more, halting me in my tracks.

It sounds like something… or someone is banging. The noise was coming from behind my house now, moving further away from where I had heard it earlier.

I slipped around the side of the house, moving the flashlight around at lightning speed. My heart was beating out of my chest.

This is stupid. There's a murderer walking around out there.

And here I was… being a complete idiot. The noise ceased once more. It was more than likely an animal that had found something to snack on and was doing so rather loudly. I might have been about to stumble upon a pack of raccoons in a garbage can.

I turned around, ready to head back in, when a high-pitched yelp made the hairs on my neck stand straight up. I started to run into the house, stumbling and dropping my flashlight, when I felt a hand grab mine.

I took a breath to scream.

"Erin! Relax, it's me." Damon's voice broke through the darkness.

"Damon? What the hell are you doing out here?" I questioned.

"I heard a loud noise and came outside to check. I saw it, though. It's those coyotes again, in the trash cans. They are getting bolder, coming from the woods into town."

Damon trailed after me, handing me the flashlight back. With the light shined on him, I could now see how disheveled his appearance was. His green eyes were even more vivid in the light, and his salt-and-pepper hair was tousled. He squared his broad, muscular shoulders to me, and I noticed he seemed on edge.

Even in a messed-up state, he's so attractive. The years have done him good.

"Are you okay?" I eyed him warily.

"What? Me? I'm fine." He smoothed his shirt and rubbed his eyes. "I was just sleeping… and I heard the noises, so I wanted to come investigate." He motioned to the yard.

"And what were you planning to do when you found someone? Fight them with your bare hands?"

I regretted it the moment I said it. Of course, Damon was capable of that. He was a retired Navy SEAL. I blamed the exhaustion and stress of the early morning.

A low chuckle rumbled from his throat, and he reached into his back waistband, retrieving a long serrated blade.

"I always come prepared. I have a lot of people to protect…" His voice trailed off as his eyes took me in from head to toe.

My stomach squeezed in a knot. I had never been looked at like that before, and especially not by Damon.

The door opened behind me, and Ellison stepped out, a pistol in his hand. He was wearing our dad's headlight, which he used for plumbing work.

"What are you two doing?" he whispered.

"What are *you* doing with a gun?!" I shrieked.

"I heard a noise. You guys heard it, too?"

"Yeah. The area's all clear, but I'll make sure to let the police know tomorrow. Will you guys be all right?" He directed the question to both my brother and me.

"Yeah, I got her. Thanks, man." Ellison shook Damon's hand and led me back inside.

He locked both the doorknob and the bolt, along with the windows, making his way throughout the house.

"What was really going on, Erin? You know you can be honest with me," my brother started as he unloaded the gun and set it on the counter.

What?

Stolen From My Billionaire Boss

"I'm not sure what you mean. I told you what happened. You said you heard the noise yourself, so I'm not sure what you're accusing me of." My arms crossed my chest in defense.

"You've always had a schoolgirl crush on him, let's be real. But you're back here for good. And now you're at his company, so you can't screw that up."

Where the hell is this coming from?

"I have done nothing to skew your trust or to give you any reason to act like this. I don't lie to you, and I never have. If this is coming from some deep-rooted insecurity that I'm not aware of, then work on that before accusing me of lying and sneaking behind your back." I pressed the flashlight into his chest, stalking off to the room.

I slammed the door behind me, cringing instantly at the noise. I didn't want to wake my parents. The door slam felt incredibly childish, and took me back to my teenage years. I don't think Ellison and I had ever had a disagreement before, and it didn't feel good.

It felt liberating to stand my ground, however. What I said was true. I had never lied to my brother before, and the accusation of sneaking around with Damon and lying about it was uncalled for.

As I lay my head on the pillow, sleep didn't feel close. But I slowly started to drift, and soon fell asleep.

Knock, knock, knock.

My eyes peeled wide open, feeling wiped from the middle-of-the-night antics I found myself in. The knocking continued, and I realized it was my bedroom door.

"Come in!" I sat up in bed.

The door swung open, and Ellison stepped in. He was

carrying a plate of fresh cinnamon rolls and a contrite look.

"I'm sorry. There isn't much more to say other than I'm sorry. I was wrong, and honestly, I don't even know where that came from. When I saw you guys out there huddled in the dark, my mind just went to a weird place." He handed me the plate, and my stomach did a happy dance.

These smell heavenly.

"And the cinnamon rolls?" I asked, popping a piece into my mouth.

"…part of the apology." He sat beside me, ogling the plate in my hand.

"Have at it."

A smile spread across my brother's face as he pulled off a piece and devoured it.

"I'm going into town today. Did you need anything?" I wanted to see all the places I used to frequent years ago. It would be nice to immerse myself in the town and relax. After all, my boss practically gave me the go-ahead himself.

"Erin… why? Unless you need something, we should all be really careful," he warned, wagging his finger in my face.

I know there's a killer. But if we all hide and cower in our homes, never allowing ourselves to enjoy our lives again… they win.

"I won't hide. Besides, it's… eight a.m. Surely, they'll be sleeping still," I said as I checked the bedside alarm clock.

"Pepper spray. And I think I'll give you my stun gun, too." Ellison started to walk out of the room.

Oh boy.

After a long lecture from my brother about the proper way to use a taser, I could leave the house. My drive into town was therapeutic, and it was easy to remember why I loved growing up here. The trees and greenery were in full bloom, with flowers aplenty and bouquets adorning most of the shops in the center of town.

Joe's Cup-A Joe was my first stop. I needed some caffeine to help me get moving after my lack of sleep.

"Just a large coffee, please," I asked the barista, pulling out my wallet.

The coffee shop was like a ghost town. It had been years, but I remembered this place being packed to the brim with a healthy line out the door. Now, it looked as if it was about to be put out of business… except for one man sitting in the corner, huddled over his drink like he was protecting it.

"What flavor?" the barista inquired.

Coffee flavor?

"Oh no, just regular coffee. Although, I'll take some milk if you have it."

"We have almond milk, oat milk, and soy milk."

I don't remember there being this many options.

"I guess oat milk… thanks."

She handed me my coffee, and I opted to sit at the window to watch people.

"Lots of coffee options, huh?" The stranger chuckled as he looked my way.

I hadn't noticed it earlier, but he had a large scar from his chin to his eyebrow, crossing over his eyelid. He couldn't have been a year or two older than I was, but he looked aged far beyond that.

"I'll say. I didn't realize there were so many milk options alone." A laugh escaped my throat.

The stranger fully turned himself towards me at this point, and I halfway thought he was about to get up and sit with me.

"I haven't seen you around. You must be new. I'm Andrew… Foley." He offered his hand.

"Erin. And no, I've lived here forever. Just moving back after a few years." My hand shook his.

"Yeah, I definitely would have noticed someone who looked like you. You're stunning."

He was flirting with me, and it was nice. Sure, he was a complete stranger, but he had a trusting nature about him. Still, I had my hand lingering near my taser in my pocket, ready to use it at a moment's notice.

"That's sweet. So, do you live in town?" It was a loaded question.

"Uh, just on the outskirts. But I love the coffee here. Well, it's been nice meeting you, but I have a busy day. See you around." He smiled as he grabbed his coffee and walked off.

Interesting.

"I'm surprised he left. He usually sits here all day," the barista commented.

I turned to respond, but she was talking to the other employee, not me.

They nodded their heads and returned to the back of the shop. I decided to take my coffee to go and stroll the streets. It was always a lot more fun to walk around versus driving through. You were more likely to miss things that way.

"Erin!" Mrs. Jones called.

My eyes cast up as I stepped out of the shop to see her hobbling over. She was well into her eighties now and had been running the flower shop since she was in her early thirties. The town had unofficially appointed her as everyone's adopted grandma. They looked after her.

"Hi, Mrs. Jones! How are you?"

"I'm okay, dear. Just hanging in there. But I wanted to

talk to you. What are you doing out and about? Didn't Ellison tell you about the murders?" Her eyes shifted back and forth.

"He did. But I can't live my life in fear. Besides, I always prepare myself." I tapped my pocket jokingly.

"Just be careful, sweetheart. There are some shifty characters lately." Her voice trailed off as she glanced behind me.

I spun around to see Andrew standing in the distance, watching us intently.

When he noticed me, he stalked off out of sight.

"Just be careful," she reiterated, returning to the flower shop.

Oh, I will.

Chapter Four

DAMON

This damn button was about to drive me insane. I had changed out of my shirt about four times, wanting to look especially good for some reason. It was fixing to make me late to work.

Today was Erin's first day of onboarding, so I had to dedicate an hour or two to give her a run-through of the system operations. When I started my company, I made it a point to be involved with welcoming all new employees. I wanted the company to feel like a family… similar to how I felt in the Navy.

Of course, Erin was already practically family by now, but tradition was as tradition does.

I slipped the jacket over my shirt and was finally ready to go.

My mind had been all out of sorts the entire morning. The nightmares had come again last night, leaving me with a measly three hours of sleep.

They had frequented me for years but recently had flared up again, making me lose focus. I was comfortable with running on low amounts of sleep; that was something I had become used to when I was a SEAL. However, it was the emotional torment the nightmares brought that was unnerving me.

This was not the time to be off my game. I had people to protect… and a job to do.

Ellison texted me as I drove to work.

El: Take care of my sister today. I think she's nervous.

Damon: She has nothing to worry about. You, on the other hand…

El: Ha-ha. I'll see you later. Have to take mom to the doctor.

Damon: Give her my love.

My eyes felt droopy. *Joe's* was coming up on the left, so I made a quick stop.

"Hi, welcome to Joes!" The barista was unusually perky as I entered.

The shop was completely empty. I wish the townspeople weren't letting the fear overtake them like this. Business owners didn't really have an option of staying closed, and the lack of monetary flow was hurting them.

"Hey, can I get a black coffee? Large, please," I asked, sliding a five-dollar bill to her.

"Coming right up!"

Just then, the door chimed behind me.

Finally, some business for poor old Joe.

I hadn't seen the man before. He raised all kinds of red flags. For one, he kept his head down the entire time he was in the shop. I turned back around, my guard fully up. As he stood behind me, I could hear him fidgeting with something. My weight shifted to one side, allowing me to glance back slightly without being too obvious.

He had a phone in his hand, an older model. The man pushed the buttons furiously, upset about something.

"Here ya go, sugar," the barista said as she handed me a steaming cup of coffee.

"Thanks, you have a good day."

"Excuse me," he mumbled as he brushed past me.

"The usual, Andrew?" she asked him, and he grumbled a response too low for me to hear.

Andrew. I'll have to look into that at work.

He pulled out an electric key and locked his car from the door of the coffee shop—a black Subaru. On the way out, I jotted down his license plate number.

A quick look at the clock told me I needed to hurry up. I suspected Erin would arrive annoyingly early for her first day of work.

My suspicions were confirmed as I pulled into the parking lot and spotted her standing in front of the entrance, nervously fixing her clothes and smoothing the skirt down.

She wore a navy-blue pencil skirt that hugged her hips, hips that I hadn't noticed until now. A matching blouse and blazer paired with the skirt, and she looked utterly… stunning. Her usually frizzy brown hair was sleek and pulled into a bun, and her green eyes shone brightly beneath her long eyelashes.

Don't go there, Damon.

"Ready to work?"

"Yes, absolutely. Good morning, boss," Erin smiled, opening the door for me.

Her demeanor had immediately shifted from the nervousness I previously observed to one of a much more confident persona. It almost had to be falsified.

"Why thank you, ma'am."

"Welcome, Mr. Clark. Good morning," Cassandra smiled.

"Thank you, you as well, Miss Alexander."

"So, Erin, today will be on boarding. A lot of it will be introducing you to the way we go through our day, how to clock in, where to find the lunch room, procedure, and all that boring stuff. Then tomorrow, we can start talking about your workload and your day-to-day," I started as the elevator whirred around us.

Her perfume smell was intoxicating. Being this close to her, just us, was driving me absolutely wild. Her arm brushed mine slightly, and I adjusted myself a few inches away.

"That sounds good. Is that with you, personally, or do I need to report somewhere?"

"Let's go to my office, and I'll get you started on the contract paperwork. We can review some of the basic things to start, and then I'll have my assistant Charles walk you through the rest. Sounds good?"

"Sure, sounds good." She looked down, rubbing her hands together.

She seems... disappointed almost.

Maybe I'm misinterpreting it. Perhaps I need to break the ice.

"Did you get back to sleep the other night? After all the ruckus?"

"Well, I had a fight with Ellison after, but surprisingly enough, I did get a little bit of sleep."

A fight with her brother? Why the hell would they be fighting?

"Can I ask why you two were fighting?"

She took a sharp intake of breath.

"About you, actually. He accused me of lying about the real reason I was out there with you."

That's absurd... and out of character for Ellison.

"That's crazy. I can only imagine he apologized after."

"Of course he did. With cinnamon rolls, nonetheless," she laughed.

"That's the only way to do it," I joined her laughter.

The elevator doors opened, and she stepped out first and then to the side.

Charles greeted us both as we stepped into my office.

"You can take a seat. It will take me a minute to get all these out." I started to fumble with the file cabinet, another massive pain in my ass.

Erin's silent giggling could be heard as I struggled with the big hunk of metal. Finally, the drawer gave, almost sending me flying back as it did.

"Here," I said, handing her a large stack. "You don't have to review it all now, but take it home. It's company policy and procedure, and your login codes will be on there. You're welcome to change passwords once you get started at the computer, but be sure to write them down. I can get you started on the tour and show you to your office."

I stood, motioning with my hand to the door. As she stood, I couldn't help but stare. Everything about her was inviting, and I mentally chastised myself. She was my friend's sister. She was my sister's best friend. She was untouchable. And yet, I found myself wanting to touch her... all over.

Get a fucking grip, man.

We circled through the floor she would be working on. I directed her through the kitchen, the bathrooms, and her office. I'd made sure that it was cleaned up the weekend prior so she could have a spot to sit that was comfortable.

"This is huge!" she exclaimed, surveying her new surroundings.

"You need a space where you can work comfortably.

We can go over your exact job description briefly before I have to get back to work and Charles will take over."

She took a seat in her new chair, leaning back with her hands behind her head, joking around.

"You look like you could be the one running this company."

"Yeah, right. I wouldn't know the first thing about running a company."

Sitting in her chair in front of the desk, I began explaining the details of her job.

"So in my line of work, we deal with mostly helping people add security to their homes, whether that be a system we can install, security features, or even, in some cases, an actual guard to sit on the premises. However, there are some private cases that only a couple of other employees and I handle. In these, people come to us because they're scared. There's someone in their life who they've encountered that leaves them turning to us to protect them. And that's where you come in," I explained.

She nodded her head, focused on what I was saying.

"You have a deep understanding of people—why they do things and what behaviors are red flags. You can help us create profiles of these people of interest, and it will help us set up better security measures for our clients."

"That sounds perfect for me."

"Yeah? Alright, good. I'm going to send Charles in to help you get your computer set up and all that. I'll check in on you later, but feel free to stop by my office with any questions. Or you can call extension three, which is a direct line to me. Good luck, Erin. Not that you'll need it." I smiled as I stepped out of her office, shutting the door behind me.

As I walked back to my office, I felt a sense of joy come over me. I think I was going to enjoy having her around.

She was a great asset to my company and very easy on the eyes.

"Charles, please get Miss Summers set up with the rest of her onboarding. I have a meeting to attend," I nodded at my assistant, who quickly jumped up.

"Right away, sir."

The rest of my day was a jumbled mess of meetings, new clients, and overseeing current clients with their security additions. Ellison had stopped in a little later and then went straight out on assignment to Miss Archer's home. She had hired a security detail for the next week since she was temporarily working from home with a busted foot.

By the end of the work day, I realized I had failed to check on Erin. I hadn't heard much else from her, not even a call. Charles had been gone for about an hour or two before returning to his desk and resuming administrative duties.

Grabbing my briefcase, I headed for her office. She was turning off the computer and collecting her things. I cleared my throat to gain her attention.

"You scared me," she said as she shot straight up, looking flustered. But then she quickly smiled.

"Sorry. How was today? You didn't seem to need any help adjusting."

I straightened my tie as I observed her. Her hair was tousled, and she looked comfortable. I wanted her to be comfortable here.

"Charles was a great help. Actually, a lot of the systems were pretty straightforward. I'm confident going into tomorrow." She flashed me a beaming grin as she stood.

"That's great to hear. Do you have anything going on tonight?"

She appeared taken aback by my question, and I wondered immediately if I had overstepped.

"No… I don't. Why?"

"Look, a couple of us were going to the GoalPosts for some drinks. A little way to kick off the week. Did you want to join?"

She pondered for a second before nodding enthusiastically.

"Great! You know how to get there still?"

"Of course, I'll meet you there."

Turning on my heel, I sped off before she could change her mind, not that I was sure she would. I was more excited than I expected that she agreed to have drinks with me.

Not with you, with her coworkers.

That's right… coworkers. It was a professional hangout with coworkers, nothing more. I guess I had to keep reminding myself that. What I couldn't understand was why Erin had started to affect me the way she had.

A mystery.

Chapter Five

ERIN

He was acting weird, but I wasn't sure if I was reading too much into it. I collected my things quickly to try and catch up to him, but by the time I stepped out of my office, he was already in the elevator heading down.

Damn.

My first day went really well. I knew in my heart that I would do an excellent job here. Being that it was Damon as my boss made it a little odd, though. He'd grown more attractive with age, and he had already looked pretty good. However, he was Cara's brother, and adding the boss factor was sealing the deal there.

"Hold the door!" Charles yelled as I stepped into the elevator. I stuck my foot out to stop the doors.

"Thanks." He slid his hand on the door, stepping in.

"Are you going to The GoalPosts with us?"

"I think so. It sounds fun," I grinned. I had always

enjoyed that bar, with its wall full of monitors showing different sports.

"Oh yeah. It's always fun. The boss usually pays, too. You did a great job for your first day. I think you'll pick things up pretty quickly." He patted me on the back.

I nodded in response as the elevator doors opened, and we stepped out.

"See you there!" I yelled over my shoulder.

The GoalPosts was a mere five-minute drive from the office, located directly behind an antique store. The layout was odd, and if you weren't a local, you would have a hard time finding the place.

I opted to leave the professional jacket behind and switch out my flats for some heels I kept in the car. As I walked in, Damon was sitting on a barstool with a glass of honey-colored liquid—likely bourbon.

He raised the glass to his lips when his eyes met mine. Damon threw the rest of it back, wiping his mouth clean. Our eyes never broke as I made my way over to him.

"You started without me?" I asked boldly.

"Ah, it's been a trying day." He flagged the bartender for another.

"Make that two." I took a seat next to him.

The tension was palpable as we sat in silence, waiting for our drinks. Coworkers piled in around us, all engaged with one another, but none made a comment or moved towards us.

As the bartender slid our drinks towards us, I found the confidence building once more.

"Hey, can I ask you something? Neighbor to neighbor, friend to friend, I guess?"

"Sure." He turned towards me.

"The other night… when we heard the noise, you looked like something had happened. Your hair was a mess, and your eyes were bloodshot…" I trailed off, hoping Damon would fill in the blanks.

The last thing I wanted was to sound accusatory.

"You're wondering what happened. It's quite a long story, probably better suited for another time. The short version, on the other hand, is that I have PTSD from the Navy. I've had recurrent nightmares since I left off and on. Lately, with the added stress from the murders, they've been a little more frequent."

My heart panged with guilt. I hated more than anything that the people who chose to serve and protect us were usually left with wounds even after service, and not always physical ones. Something I learned in behavior theory was tell-tale signs of PTSD and how, for some, it felt as if they were still serving.

Without thinking, I reached out to embrace him in a hug. Damon's body hardened under my touch for a few seconds, then his arm wrapped around my lower body, and he hugged me back.

"Well, don't you two look cozy?" Cara's voice filled the space, breaking us out of our embrace.

"Cara!" I squealed, jumping out of my seat.

We squeezed the life out of each other. I hadn't gotten much of a chance to see her since I had been back between her working such crazy hours and watching her kids.

"Erin! College did you good, girl. You look stunning! Doesn't she look stunning, Damon?"

"Yes, she does." Damon lifted his glass.

"Come over here and catch up with me." She pulled me off to the side, completely disregarding her brother.

We sat together as she ordered an apple martini. She was the same Cara as always, and it was refreshing to see she hadn't lost herself. The memory of us crafting cocktails at the ripe age of sixteen in the garage of her parents' house started flooding back as she took a sip.

That was the most fun I had back then. I was otherwise reserved, but not when it came to Cara.

"How are the kids? How's the husband?"

"The kids are insane. They're wonderful and fulfilling… but insane. Jonas has been so busy with work that I hardly see him most nights. We're in an *off* phase, if you know what I mean. He hasn't been interested in anything intimate," she confessed, sadness flitting across her face.

I can't imagine how that would make me feel.

"I'm sorry. Have you talked to him about it?"

"Yeah, and he says it's the stress from work. He says he'll be okay once he gets a break," Cara sighed.

"I don't know what to say. Maybe give him time, maybe get a sitter so you can carve out alone time when he's off work?"

"You know anybody willing?" She giggled.

"Me, of course. I'd love to watch them. What are they doing tonight?"

"At home, waiting for me to come back. Some days, you need an after-work drink before you face the madness. Want to come for dinner? It's meatloaf night."

It would feel good to be around family.

"Absolutely. Let's go." We both knocked back the rest of our drinks.

I waved goodbye to Damon and the rest of my coworkers as we left together.

"Meet you there. I'll text you my address now." She waved me off as I got into my car.

Once in the car, I got the oddest feeling of being watched. It was starting to get dark out, but with the neon of the bar paired with the street lights, I could still see. There was nobody around.

Except for someone standing off by the trash cans. He had his head down, so I couldn't see his face.

This is ballsy. But I have to see.

My hand shook as I switched on the car's lights. The man lifted his head in shock, and I could see his face clearly in the glow of the neon lights.

It's Andrew.

I held up an apologetic hand and backed out of the parking lot.

What was he doing there? Why was he hanging around outside like that?

I had no time to try and answer those questions as my car pulled into Cara's driveway. It was the first time I had been to her new house, and it was breathtaking. It was a two-story farmhouse-style home with a cobblestone driveway. Toys scattered the front yard, along with a swing set.

She had pulled in right before me.

"The kids will be so excited to see you!" She opened the door.

"Mommy!" her daughter, Lila, screamed as she ran into her open arms. Jonas put their son down, who immediately began to crawl excitedly towards his mother. Jonas, on the other hand, had a grim look. He eyed me warily, then smiled.

"Hi, Erin. It's nice to see you." He pulled me in for a tight hug as I side-eyed Cara.

Hugging me before his wife?

"Hey, babe." He grabbed her, pulling her into a quick embrace before stalking off.

"Yup," Cara mouthed as we moved into the family room.

She left the kids with me as she started to prepare dinner. Luke was sitting on my lap as he chewed on toy after toy, and Lila was busy at work coloring pictures. She had a stack of them to the side already done.

"Did you already do these? They look beautiful! Can I see them?"

"Sure!" Lila handed me the stack.

As I flipped through her drawings, I found myself impressed with her artistic ability. There were pictures of flowers, animals, and princesses with so much detail that it would put me to shame if I tried. The last picture made my heart drop, however. If she weren't such a good artist, I would be confused about what it was. It depicted a very gruesome image, with multiple people lying on the ground and blood surrounding them.

"Honey, what's this?" I asked.

She looked up at the drawing in my hand, shrugged her shoulders, and returned to the image she was working on.

"I'll be right back." I patted her shoulder as I made a path to the kitchen.

"Hey, she kicked you out already?" Cara laughed as she cut carrots.

"I wanted to show you this." I slid the picture over to her.

Her eyebrows furrowed in confusion and worry, then raised in surprise as she looked at the paper before her.

"What about it?" She returned to her chopping.

"It seems rather graphic for a little girl. Doesn't it worry you?"

She shrugged her shoulders nonchalantly.

"She's a little kid who likes scary movies. What do you want me to do, Erin?" She turned defensive.

Something is going on with her. But how do I tell my best friend that?

"In my line of work, that would be a red flag of an indicator that something else may be going on."

She set the knife down.

"Oh, please. As much respect as I have for you and your job, don't turn this into that. What? A kid has something going on at home because they draw a scary picture? Now it's mommy and daddy's fault? Get off your high horse, Erin," she spat.

Her words cut through me like a knife. We had spats growing up, but nothing like this.

Then again, she's just protecting her child. A mother's worry and ferocity knows no bounds.

"I'm not saying anything to that level. I was just expressing concern… as your best friend."

"As my best friend… back the hell off."

"Okay, you got it. If you don't mind, I'm tired. I think I'll take a rain check on dinner," I said. I sat Luke in his walker and walked out.

"Bye, Lila. Enjoy your evening," I called to her as I closed the door behind me.

Screw her. How dare she speak to me like that? I've never talked down to her like that… nor would I ever.

As I stormed inside the house, my mom and dad both jumped up to greet me.

"How was your first day? Why are you back so late?" They began to pepper questions at me, and I was in no mood for it.

"Not now." I held a hand up and stomped up the stairs.

I was too angry to talk to anybody.

As I grabbed the blinds to pull them down, I spotted Damon pacing back and forth in his room. He looked worried about something. Suddenly, he grabbed a stack of papers and sat down to read them. He angrily flipped through one after the other, crumpling and tossing them to the side as he did.

What's going on with him?

He looked straight up, then directly at me. Taken aback, I tried to recover with a small smile and a wave.

"You okay?" I mouthed.

He gave me a quick nod before closing his shutters.

Weird.

Maybe it was a good night to stay away from the Clark family. I'd had my fill of the crazy antics for one night.

I had enough of it for the evening. All I wanted was to get some sleep, forget about it, and start fresh in the morning.

As I drifted off to sleep, my mind replayed the day's images, but I kept returning to Lila's horrifying drawing.

I couldn't stop thinking about it.

Chapter Six

DAMON

My sister was furious, and that was something I didn't observe often. She called me this morning to discuss her and Erin's fight. Cara wouldn't tell me the reason and was very coy when I tried to ask. I knew what it was about, though. She had seen us together at the bar and read something into it. Erin was her best friend, and I could see how she wouldn't want anything to happen between her brother and her.

I held my tongue on the phone call, focusing more on my niece and nephew. The fight would pass; it always did… although the two of them rarely fought.

It was my second day of work with Erin, and I found myself happily expecting to see her. But I needed to rein it in. If Cara was mad enough about suspecting something between her friend and me, that was even more of a reason to keep things professional.

I rounded out the door as I fastened the final button on

my shirt. Erin was walking down the steps as I closed the door behind me, and she looked beautiful. Her usually messy hair was neatly tied back in a bun atop her head, and she wore a pantsuit that hugged every curve of her body.

Jesus.

"Fancy running into you here!" she shouted as she climbed into the car.

"See you at work." I waved to her as I climbed into my truck.

My phone rang as I pulled out of the driveway, right behind Erin.

"Hey, Mom. What's going on?"

"Hello, dear. Your father and I wanted to call and see if you had any updates on the murders. I know you must think we're silly to skip town, but it's a little unnerving."

"There are no updates, unfortunately. They are no closer to finding the killer… and neither am I. And you know how I feel about you guys leaving. I would have protected you, but I can understand the fear."

"I was worried that was the case. Dad wants to know how Erin is doing at the company. Your sister mentioned you hired her. We're thrilled! You know we've always loved her."

"It's her second day, but I think she'll be great. I'm almost to work, so I'm going to have to let you go. I love you. I'll call you later," I said, pulling into the parking lot.

"Okay, my love. Have a good day."

The phone call ended as I collected my things before climbing out of the truck.

"Hey, stranger. You following me?" Erin joked as she breezed up.

"You wish. Ready for your second day?"

"Absolutely." She stepped in as I opened the door for her.

Everyone was in a frenzy as we walked inside. My receptionist, Cassandra, was taking phone call after phone call.

What's going on?

Erin and I entered the elevator as the doors closed around us. Like a switch, the air grew heavy between us. Her phone began to ring in her purse, and she fumbled for it before dropping her bag on the floor.

"Shit," she bent to grab it.

"I got it—" I leaned down at the same time.

Our hands grazed as we both reached for the purse. She pulled her hand back quickly as a reflex.

"Here." I handed it to her.

The elevator opened as my body was still reeling from her touch. It was as if every nerve were amplified, searing from the contact.

"Hello?" Erin answered her phone, following me out of the elevator.

My employees looked panicked. That only meant one thing.

There was another murder. That, or they caught the killer, which I highly doubted.

"I will." Erin hung up the phone.

Her hand brushed lightly against my back as she leaned in close.

"There was another murder. My mom said to turn on the news. She's completely freaked out," Erin confirmed, sliding her phone back into her purse.

All I could think about was her hand on my back and all the things I would do to her if this weren't going on.

Stepping to the side, I gestured for us to go into my office. The news lit up as I switched the television on.

"We are saddened to report the loss of another life in our community. Allison Davis was found dead this morning in her home. We have not received the cause of death, but we have confirmed it is directly related to the recent string of murders. Miss Davis was employed at *Joe's Coffee Shop*, a town favorite…" the news anchor trailed off.

I just saw her yesterday.

Erin's face paled as she listened to the report. I switched the TV off. I would be receiving reports soon enough anyway.

"Erin?"

She turned to me, tears in her eyes. Her hand covered her mouth in shock.

"I just saw this woman. I was there. It could've been me. It could've just as easily been me," she sputtered.

Everything in me wanted to comfort her. But my sister wouldn't have liked that. She clearly had an issue with the idea of Erin and I, not that there really was an "Erin and I" at this point.

I rubbed her back as she took big, deep breaths to steady herself. I knew how terrifying it was to everyone.

Be professional… as hard as it is.

My arms released her as I stepped back, gripping the edge of my desk for support. It was getting harder and harder to resist the way she was making me feel—the way being around her was making me feel.

Erin wiped her eyes, collecting herself.

"Sorry about that. This is all… a lot," she apologized.

"Believe me, I understand. Uh… I should probably get started," I said, gesturing to the growing pile of work.

Please take the hint.

"Right. Well, I'll go click in. Sorry again about that."

I didn't look up as I heard the door softly shut. I wanted to pull her in, make her feel safe. She still held the doe-eyed innocence she always had, but now she was mature, strong, and confident. It was a refreshing change of pace that was a stark contrast to the little girl I used to know growing up.

The internal struggle brewing since I had first seen her after her return was growing impossible to ignore, yet not something I could face head-on. So many factors went into precisely why telling her how I felt was a bad idea. For one, it was clear my sister wasn't a fan of the idea. Two, she was an employee, and I wanted to be the kind of person who could pride myself on my workplace values, including not dating the staff. And last, our families had too close of a relationship to possibly skew that by pursuing something with Erin. The way Ellison reacted the other night when he saw us together spoke volumes.

Besides, I wasn't sure if Erin felt the same way. I didn't think she did at all. But it was better that way. It was the only way.

My day felt monotonous—one case after the other. Phone calls, scheduling, ordering security systems, and so forth.

My work email pinged with a new message notification. It was from Erin.

From: Erin.summers@workspace.org
To: dclark@workspace.org
Subject: Checking in…

I'm sure your day has been just as busy as mine. I just wanted to check in and see if you were doing okay. I'm here if you need anything.

-Erin

What a breath of fresh air. It was a pleasant surprise.

From: dclark@workspace.org
To: Erin.summers@workspace.org
Subject: Checking in…Work has been quite dull. It's nice to get a

friendly message, though. How are you doing? I know this morning was quite a shock.

Her response was immediate. It came through the direct chat box, however.

Erin S: Figured the chat box would be better. It was a shock. I had just seen her. Something was off about this guy I ran into at the shop as well. He just lingered there.

My blood ran cold.

Damon C: What guy? Tell me.

Erin S: His name was Andrew. That's all I know. Well, I should get going. Thanks for this… brightened my day. See you tomorrow.

It brightened my day, too. Her user ID quickly turned off, and I decided to call it a night as well. Maybe if I was quick enough, I could catch her in the elevator.

Sure enough, there she was as I stepped out of my door, waiting for the elevator. Her hair was undone and lingering past her shoulders, a chocolate mess of waves and frizz. It was inviting and made me want to wrap my hands in it.

"Hold the door, please." I sauntered over, not wanting to let my true feelings be known.

Play it cool.

The air became charged and full of tension as the doors closed around us and the elevator slowly descended. She peeked at me through her hair, and my body tensed in response.

Does she want this, too?

"I'm sorry if my sister suspected anything about us when she came out. It wasn't my intention for you two to fight," I apologized.

She immediately hit the stop button on the elevator, forcing it to cease movement.

"What are you talking about?" she questioned, clearly bewildered.

"Cara. She said you two had a fight. I figured it was about us. Was it not?"

"No… it was about something I shouldn't have expressed concern over. I can explain that later. Why would you think she thought there was something between us?" She eyed me up and down, and I knew right then it wasn't one-sided.

Tell her.

I wanted to, but it felt selfish to put it out there. Putting the attraction out there meant disturbing a work relationship that was off to a great start and putting her brother's suspicions to fruition.

Fuck it.

"Isn't there?" I leaned back against the wall, folding my arms across my chest matter-of-factly.

The air left her lungs as she surveyed me nervously. Newfound confidence aside, it was apparent she never thought anything would transpire between us. But I couldn't help but confess. Keeping the way I felt bottled up was screwing with my head, and I needed my focus these days. For all I knew, she would turn me down, and then I could relax, knowing that it was her choice… that I spoke the truth, and it wasn't enough.

Suddenly, her posture shifted, and she stood straight, glowing with confidence. She slowly walked over to me, placing her hand on my chest.

This feels good.

"Damon… you're my boss. I—"

I cut her off, pushing her against the wall. Our lips tangled in a heated mess of need and desperation. Her hands threaded through my hair, giving it a gentle tug. Her tongue searched for mine as I gripped her ass, lifting her against the wall.

It was more than I had imagined, and I wanted all of her right then and there.

Erin's hands moved from my hair to the sides of my face as we kissed in a synchronous movement of lust. I kissed her like she was air, and I couldn't breathe. I needed it.

She was the first to break the kiss, stepping back quickly... as if she had to force herself.

"That was..." She touched her lips like they were on fire.

I know, baby. I know.

"Yeah..." I breathed in agreement as I hit the stop button again, resuming movement.

We sat silently as the elevator descended, both at a loss for words. As the doors opened, we stood still. Erin turned to me, a pained look on her face.

"It can't happen again," she said as she hurried out.

And then she was gone.

Chapter Seven

ERIN

I could feel his fiery kisses lingering on my lips. It was single-handedly the best kiss I had ever experienced in my life.

No one had ever kissed or touched me like that before.

Damon Clark was unlike anyone I had ever known. He was accomplished, kind, intelligent, and sexy. I had always thought he was handsome, even as a kid. But he was way older, and I doubt he ever saw me in that way. Until now, of course. The age gap had always been an issue until both were adults, and then it didn't seem to matter.

Surprisingly, I wasn't worried about the work or family dynamic being altered by our kiss. I told him it couldn't happen again and bolted before he could answer… or before I could see his face.

The one thing that plagued me as we were kissing and the quiet moments that followed was the sobering truth: Damon Carter could break my heart into a thousand pieces. He was the one man who could genuinely hurt me. Growing up, I had always found him attractive, but there was never any actual yearning. I knew that I could never have him. He was older, and he was my friend's brother. We couldn't go there, only for it to be taken away. That couldn't happen.

So I told him no, even though every nerve in my body was screaming yes.

I left the parking log before he emerged. I was taking the cowardly way out, and I knew it. It didn't stop me, however.

My phone rang.

I looked down. It was Cara.

"Hello?" My voice was full of worry, knowing I was probably about to receive another verbal lashing.

"I'm sorry," she spilled out.

"Me too. I wanted to call you and tell you that last night, but I thought it was too soon. You're my best friend, and I would never do anything to mess that up."

"Oh, please. The friendship is going to the grave. Look, I have a lot of tension with my husband right now, and I took some of that out on you. It wasn't fair. The truth is, Lila's drawings are terrifying, but she sees me and her dad fight a lot. She likes scary movies, and I don't want to be the one to take that away. Can you come over? We can have the dinner I promised you."

Yes. I need to take my mind off of what just happened.

"I'll be right there."

I sped to her house, definitely going over the speed limit. A distraction was what I needed.

As I knocked on the door, Jonas swung the door open with a smile. His demeanor was a three-sixty from what I had experienced the day before.

"Erin. Cara said you would be joining us for dinner. I

wanted to apologize firsthand for my coolness the other evening. There's been a lot going on."

"I understand, and there's no need to apologize; I'm just happy to be invited." I smiled as he stepped aside to allow me in.

"You're back!" Lila squealed as she jumped into my arms.

I mainly had seen her through a series of FaceTimes over the years, but seeing her in person was even better. She looked so much like her mom did as a child, and it took me back to when we were kids.

"Hi, sweetheart! Let me check that out." I pointed to the drawing in her hand.

As she handed it to me, I couldn't help but smile. It was a picture of me surrounded by flowers. She was a talented artist for her age, but the frizzy brown hair gave it away.

"Dinner's served!" Cara shouted.

"Hi, my darling. Let's not fight again." Cara embraced me tightly, releasing me once her husband sauntered in.

"Hey, baby. Work done?" she asked as he planted a tender kiss on her lips.

They've done a three-sixty too.

Eyeing her carefully, she met my gaze with a wink, meaning she would fill me in later. Dinner this evening was a pot roast with roasted vegetables and mashed potatoes.

I'm drooling.

We all sat, and Cara fastened Luke into his high chair. His chubby cheeks danced with delight as she piled some of everything onto his tray. He was all about "baby-led weaning," which allowed him to eat like the rest of the family versus purées. According to Cara, it was all the rage.

"So Jonas, work has been tough lately?" I pried, wanting to figure out the reason for his bad mood as of late.

"You have no idea. My boss has been riding my ass for the past few weeks, but I finally got a promotion this morning. It's like a weight lifted off of my shoulders." He popped a piece of meat into his mouth, grabbing Cara's hand with a gentle squeeze.

"That's wonderful."

"What about you? Cara tells me that you're working for Damon. What's that like? He cracking the whip?" He laughed.

"Uncle Damon!" Lila giggled as she devoured her potatoes.

"He's not the dictator you might think. It's a dream job. I'm enjoying it." I smiled.

And enjoying him.

"I'm glad you like it. I'm sure my brother enjoys having you around. I know he admired you for getting an advanced degree like that. He'll never admit it, of course," Cara confessed.

"That's nice to hear. But talk about him—he's served. That's something to admire."

"Indeed it is," Jonas agreed.

The meal was enjoyed as we reminisced on our teenage years. Cara and I had the best time together back then, even though I had my nose shoved in a book most of the time, as she so poetically put it.

Even though no guy ever noticed me.

"Anyone up for dessert?" Cara offered, clearing the plates.

"Sounds wonderful. Here, let me help you." I grabbed mine and Lila's plates, following her to the kitchen.

"Spill. Jonas seems so much better today," I said, nudging Cara's arm.

She smiled, turning on the sink to rinse the dishes.

"It's true. I confronted him this morning right after he

received the call from his boss. It's been a complete switch since then. I guess I was reading too much into it."

Making my way around the counter, I pulled her into me, "That makes me happy to hear."

We tucked into dessert, a delicious combination of fresh berries and homemade whipped cream. I excused myself shortly after to make my way home and relax. It had been a draining day mentally, and nothing screamed unwind more like a feel-good movie.

As I started my car, my phone started to buzz repeatedly with a series of texts. They were all from the same unknown number.

You look beautiful today.
Be careful out at night. There's a murderer out.
Guess who?
I'll see you soon.

My stomach churned as I read the last message. I hoped it was some kind of sick joke being played by a teenager with tons of time on their hands. Still, better to be safe than sorry. I took a screenshot and emailed it to the tip line at the police department.

Pulling into my parents' driveway, I saw that Damon was home, and the light in his room was on. A large part of me wanted to knock on the door and pick up where we left off. The other half of me just wanted to take a beat for the day because my head was still reeling from what transpired earlier.

"How was dinner at Cara's? Did you two make up?" My mom started on the inquisition as I shut the door behind me.

"It was fun. We did make up, of course. What did you guys do tonight?"

"Ellison went out with some friends for drinks at this bar. He's still out, but has been sending me hourly updates.

You know how I worry. But your dad and I had some much-needed alone time, if you know what I mean…" she trailed off, her eyes fixed on my dad asleep on the couch.

Gross.

"That's a little more information than I needed, Mom. I'm going to retire for the night and watch a movie. I'll be in my room if you need me. I love you." I planted a kiss on her head and beelined to my room.

A quick shower and a fresh set of pajamas kickstarted the day's exhaustion. Finishing a movie didn't feel feasible, but I turned the TV on anyway. *The Notebook* was playing and had just started.

That's perfect.

I saw a shadow out of the corner of my eye through the window. Jumping up, I could see Damon pacing around the room. He stopped when he saw me standing there and waved awkwardly. I returned the favor and then pointed to my phone. Damon grabbed his and called me.

"What's going on?" He breathed into the phone.

"Check your texts," I commanded, sending him the image of the texts I had received.

I was out on speakerphone as his eyes scanned his phone. He went wide-eyed, panicked, then angry.

"Who sent you these? When did you get them?" He started to bark questions into the phone, sounding like a drill sergeant.

"Damon, I don't know. I already sent them over to the police. But I wanted to let you know, because… well, I don't know. I just wanted to tell you."

"Erin, you're going to be okay. This is probably just some punk playing games. I won't let anything happen to you, I promise."

"I know. See you tomorrow?"

"Tomorrow. Goodnight, Erin." Damon turned to face me through the window.

"Goodnight, Damon."

I was the first to hang up the phone, but Damon lingered with it in his hand as he stared at me. The tension was palpable, even as we were in different rooms.

This can't work. But I want it.

Turning away, I pressed play on the television and relaxed into the bed.

My eyes were slowly closing as I fought the urge to fall asleep. The movie was nearly over, and the ending was always my favorite part. I could hear a slight knocking. Hitting pause on the movie, I cracked my bedroom door open.

"Mom? Dad?"

I was met with my mother and father's joint snoring floating from their bedroom.

"Ellison?"

No answer. The knocking grew louder, and I realized it was coming from the front door. Checking my clock, the time read nearly midnight. Maybe my brother forgot his keys. Skipping two steps at a time, I ran down the stairs quickly. The knocking ceased right as I came to a screeching halt in front of the door. I peered out of the peephole, but couldn't see anyone around. Maybe he went to Damon's house to get an answer.

Be careful.

I checked once more, then decided to slowly crack the door open. My head poked out, and I glanced side to side, but the coast was clear. Sitting in front of my feet was a white sheet of paper.

What the hell?

Once I picked it up and flipped it over, I saw it was one

of Lila's drawings. Not only that, but it was the gruesome drawing I had raised concerns over.

What the hell was it doing here? I quickly shut the door behind me and locked it, adding the deadbolt. My feet begrudgingly climbed the stairs as I mulled over all the possibilities before finally landing on the scariest one.

The paper was a warning meant only for me. This person could see me at any time. They could get into any place, whenever they wanted. It was a threat, and yet I didn't know why.

All I knew was that I was a target, and I had to watch my back.

Chapter Eight

DAMON

It couldn't happen again. We had to keep things professional. But god, that kiss. It was unlike anything I'd ever experienced before. The raw need, want, desire... it surprised even me. It would be next to impossible to see her as anything even remotely professional or in the realm of platonic.

She was wildly attractive, intelligent, and infuriating. I mean... who kissed someone like that and then tells them it can never happen again? I felt like I was losing my mind, and Erin hightailed it out of there before I could say anything else.

It felt inherently wrong to reach out about it when she made her feelings pretty clear. Besides, I saw Cara's photos on social media. Erin had gone over for dinner, so it was a really bad time to ask her about things. I knew they would make up eventually, as they were far too good of friends ever to stop talking for good.

The rest of the week of the office was painfully dull. Erin didn't talk to me unless it concerned work, and surprisingly enough, it wasn't lessening my attraction. It only made me want to take it out on the gym to get my frustration out. It was a great thing for security: pent-up aggression and tension.

I'd love to take it out on someone else, though… in the bedroom.

By Saturday morning, I felt a little bit grateful that I wouldn't be forced to see her every single day and not be able to do a damn thing about it. I would busy myself in the town doing otherwise by finding things to do.

First thing on the agenda was to hit the grocery store. My fridge was practically empty. As I arrived at the store, everyone in town was shockingly out and about. It had felt like a ghost town for quite some time, so seeing so many residents at once was a surprise.

I bumped into someone as I tried to shoulder my way past the crowd.

"I'm sorry, man," I blurted an apology out as the stranger lifted his head.

Johnny.

"Yeah, you better say sorry, you dick." He folded the weekly ad and put it into his back pocket.

"What are you going to do about it?" I folded my arms across my chest.

"Man, it's been a long time. It's good to see you." Johnny pulled me in for a tight hug.

He was my buddy from my stint in the Navy, and it had been years since I'd seen him. Last I heard, he was living in Tennessee with his wife and a baby on the way. That was about five years ago.

"What are you doing all the way out here?" We turned to browse the aisles.

"It's kind of a long story. The short version is that I

have a job in town." He shifted his head to the side, avoiding the question with a vague answer.

"What kind of job?" I pried, knowing full well he wouldn't answer.

"You know the deal, man. It's confidential. I promise I won't get in your hair too much." He ruffled my hair as he threw a box of macaroni and cheese into his cart.

Yeah, sure.

We shot the shit about our life as we browsed aisle by aisle. According to him, his wife was now his ex-wife, but he had a beautiful four-year-old daughter who was the center of his world. His ex-wife was a "vindictive bitch" who was making his life miserable.

As good as it was to see him again, he was a long way from the laid-back man I once knew as my best friend. He didn't smile much, and when he did, it felt forced. The only genuine smile I had observed the whole time was when he showed me photos of his daughter, Katherine.

"That'll be one-hundred sixteen dollars and forty-one cents," the cashier prompted, pointing to the credit card machine.

Man, this is getting expensive.

I swiped my card and swapped current numbers with Johnny before I excused myself and went to the car. My mind felt weird after our exchange. I couldn't shake the feeling that he was hiding something from me. Of course, after years of not seeing each other, he didn't owe me anything. The years did have a way of changing people, but I didn't recognize my friend, physical appearance aside. But he was in my town, and there was a murderer on the loose.

That reminds me… Andrew.

Erin had mentioned someone named Andrew who was lingering in the coffee shop and might be of interest in the murder of the barista. I had his name on my list, but I had to delve more into it today after my errands.

The investigation had been slow-moving... almost stagnant. And that was the police efforts. I had been sharing every piece of evidence I obtained with the station. However, they weren't able to do much of it. Surveillance was my forte, and I could optimize that when doing my own digging.

Not a single soul was aware of my side investigation into the murders. I wanted to keep it that way. The way I saw it, the killer was living amongst us, a wolf in sheep's clothing. As wonderful as it was financially for me with the additional business it brought, it felt wrong. I shouldn't make a profit because someone was scaring the townspeople. I had to do something, because I had experience dealing with dangerous people.

However, it was hard to find clues. The killer wasn't meticulous, which generally meant mistakes were made. But, they never picked a woman similar in age, appearance, or even job.

If I overplayed my hand too early, I would fail. Failing wasn't something I was comfortable with or accepted.

My head hurts.

The drive home was a blur. I was being wracked with my thoughts, and I couldn't focus. Maybe it was best to put my errands to the side for a few hours so I could get some much-needed rest. My nightmares had been nonstop and relentless for the last few weeks. Sleep had become a thing of the past.

The last time they got this bad, the doctor prescribed me a sleep aid. I couldn't allow myself to take them, though. There were too many horror stories of people who left the service only to dull their PTSD and pain with medication that ended up spiraling out of control.

I tried my best to allow myself to relax as I flipped through all the evidence I had collected from the murders. I had another old SEAL buddy who occasionally looked something up for me, and it helped some. The only correlations so far, according to my buddy, were bruising on the limbs and dirty fingernails. He said they had probably been tied up somehow. This person was coming to their homes, so they had some semblance of a plan as well.

Knock, knock.

The doorbell rang swiftly. Using every ounce of strength, I pulled my exhausted body off the couch and shuffled to the front door.

Erin was standing there in a light-blue sundress adorned with white flowers. She was looking jaw-dropping beautiful. In her hands were white sheets of paper.

"What did I do to deserve your company?" I smiled, swinging the door open.

She took a sharp intake of breath as she scanned me from head to toe. Erin handed me the papers as she stepped inside, pushing past me.

"These."

They were the text messages she sent me, followed by a reverse phone search result on the phone number. It was from a burner phone with no registered owner name. There was only the location. They were here.

It didn't come as a shock to me. All along, I knew the killer was living among us, just lurking in the shadows.

"You showed me these. What's going on?"

"I know I did. But read them again. Doesn't something sound off to you?" She took a seat on my couch, and I wanted nothing more than to take her right there.

However, she was upset. And she'd made her feelings obvious.

"I mean, they sound a little mundane, I guess. As far as

threats go, they're more lax than most."

I didn't know what to say. They were something to keep an eye on but not something I would lose sleep over. I wanted to tell her what she wanted to hear.

"I guess. I don't know. Maybe I'm reading more into this than I should. I'm just totally freaked out by all of this." She put her face in her hands.

Sitting next to her, I put my hand on the small of her back. Her back tensed underneath my touch, but then she sat up straight.

"I should go. This is all… I'm sorry. It won't happen again." She started for the door.

"Wait, Erin." I reached for her wrist, but she slipped from my grasp.

"The police haven't gotten back to me. And there's no work today. I think I'm letting my mind wander too much. I think I'll go to the gym or something. Maybe it can help take my mind off things."

That sounds like a good idea.

"I get it. I promise you, you'll be okay. I'll keep you safe. But I've been wanting to go work off some stress, too. I have a buddy pass for the gym. Want to join?"

Her feet shifted as she leaned to the side, pondering the offer.

"Sure, why not? Let me go get changed, and I'll follow you there."

"Deal."

She shut the door behind her softly, and I climbed the stairs two at a time, quickly getting myself dressed. The internal battle in my head between what I was doing versus what I should do was raging on. I knew that keeping things platonic and professional would be all the harder when we hung out outside the workplace.

But honestly, I saw a friend in need at that moment.

Despite my sudden and shocking feelings for her, I did have a fondness and love for her outside of that. She was like a member of the family, and she had been my sister's closest friend for so long. If she was scared and stressed, and if I could do something to alleviate that, then I would.

Because Erin wasn't a piece of meat for me. She wasn't a conquest. She was a kind, generous person, and deserving of everything this life had to offer. I don't think I was the person for her. It would cause too many complications. I could show her my friendship, though, and my loyalty. She needed that right now, and it was my duty.

Sitting in my car waiting for Erin to emerge, I thought I could do a quick information search on the mysterious "Andrew."

Nothing immediately popped up, so I plugged in my town coordinates.

Andrew James, 816 Percy Lane. 310-327-7728.

Perfect. I took a screenshot of his name and information just as Erin emerged. A time would need to be set aside later for a deep dive on him. Erin's intuition about people and behavior was something to bet everything on. She was rarely wrong; I remember that, even when she was younger. If she had an off feeling about this guy, it was something worth exploring.

She flashed me a thumbs up as she climbed into her Jeep, following me out onto the street. We quickly made our way to the gym, signed in, and went our separate ways for a little bit to work on different things. She headed for the stair machine as I went to the treadmill to warm up. Finally, she met me back by the weight rack.

"Hey, you done?" I eyed her, sweat pouring off of her like a faucet.

"Please… I'm just getting started." Erin picked up a weight.

Chapter Nine

ERIN

I made things clear.

We were to be professional and cordial. But it was hard. I found myself wanting to confide in Damon, wanting to entrust him with things that I struggled with. Of course, I had Cara. But over the years, I have felt less and less inclined to share troubling things with her. It wasn't due to a lack of love, connection, or even a dying friendship. It was none of those.

She had kids, a husband, and a family. It felt selfish to burden her with my troubles. In college, I went through something pretty traumatic. I told nobody, not even one of my family members. Instead, I buried the pain. The grief of that day was with me every single day.

Damon was holding true to my decision. He hadn't made a move since. He was the perfect gentleman. At the gym, he was perfectly normal, like friends. Come Monday, he was cold and distant.

Now, Wednesday, I felt so inclined as to ask him why. Friends, at the very least, talked, were cordial, and exchanged a few words here and there. I was lucky to get a hello or goodbye this week.

I must have done something.

Or maybe he decided to take my decision seriously. Maybe he decided it was better to ditch a relationship altogether, even one that was strictly friendship.

"Hey, Charles. Are you heading to the bar tonight?" I asked, slipping into the elevator next to him.

"Sure am. You're coming, right?" He grinned, and it was only then that I noticed how attractive he was. He had a boyish charm, with cutting green eyes and blond hair.

"Absolutely. I'll be there in thirty," I promised, hitting the close door button.

There was a change of clothes in my car. Maybe going out with my new coworkers and having fun was a great idea. I told Damon that I wanted us to be cordial. I couldn't be pining over him anymore. The choice was made, and the decision was final. It was time to put my distractions elsewhere.

Work had kept me impressively busy, but the after-hours were where I found myself trying to stay dutiful. There were no new texts and no further threats. I was at a standstill.

A mini dress, sweet.

Snatching the outfit from the trunk of my car, I hurried back into the building to the lobby floor restroom to change my clothes.

A fresh swipe of lipstick, and I was ready to go.

"Going out?" Cassandra laughed as she packed up her purse.

"Yes, ma'am. You?"

"Can't. I have to relieve the babysitter. You have fun,

though. You deserve it." She squeezed my shoulder, moving past me.

Erin: I'm going to the bar with my coworkers. Don't wait up for me, I'm okay.

Mom: No drinking and driving. Be safe. Please. Pepper spray on you?

Erin: I would never. Yes, I have it on me. No, I don't need another demonstration.

The phone chimed with an incoming text message as I turned into the parking lot of The GoalPosts bar.

Oh god, Mom. I'm okay.

It wasn't her.

Have fun. You look great.

It was from an unknown number.

My eyes quickly darted from side to side. There was no one around. My rearview mirror caught a car slowly approaching with the high beam lights on. As it grew closer and closer, my hand found the handle of the pepper spray, readying it in case I needed it.

The car made a sharp left turn and out of the parking lot. They were gone as soon as they came.

It was probably a wrong turn. Relax, Erin.

A drink should do the trick.

The bar was full of excitement and people releasing the day's stress through music, dance, and alcohol.

"Erin!" Charles shouted over the roar of the music.

He made his way to me with a shot in his hand. I guess he decided to get the party started already.

"Here you go. On Damon, of course." He laughed, knocking it back.

Damon? He's here?

"Where is he?" I looked around apprehensively before swallowing the warm amber liquid.

It burned as it went down my throat.

"Oh, I don't think he's coming today. But he always leaves his card on the tab for us. So drink up, and enjoy! By the way, with the risk of sounding like a complete tool, may I say that you look gorgeous?" Charles's gaze was intense, his eyes licking me up and down.

This feels uncomfortable.

"Thank you, Charles. I'll never turn down a compliment."

He turned away to talk to some friends, and I had never felt more grateful for an interruption in my life. I wasn't entirely sure why his compliment and attention made me uncomfortable, but all I knew was that it did.

Maybe because he's not Damon.

Damon wasn't the one for me, either. He couldn't be. Besides, I should be worrying about the person sending me ominous text messages in the wake of a string of murders.

They were taunting me… but why?

My phone began to vibrate, and I rolled my eyes.

Either mom or a deranged person… take my pick.

It was neither.

Damon: He's right, you look gorgeous.

My head spun so quickly that I nearly threw myself off balance, my heels slightly stumbling as I gripped the bar for support.

"Easy there, I think we should cut you off," Damon chuckled, helping me onto a bar stool.

"Nobody thought you were coming." I flagged the bartender down for another shot.

"Oh? Were you betting on that?"

I could feel my confidence building with every passing moment. It was most definitely the alcohol, but I didn't care.

"Stop with the coyness. You're the one who's been cold

and distant. You kiss me like that and then treat me like a stranger? What do you call that?"

His face paled at my accusation. Recovering quickly, he leaned close and whispered in my ear.

"You're the one who made the rules here. I'm just following your rules."

I couldn't do anything but shake my head. It was true, but he was taking it to an extreme. I told him to keep it professional, but he took that to mean that he should ignore me and pretend I didn't exist. The two were not mutually exclusive.

"You're going above and beyond, and you know it. We've always been friends… cordial. Why? Tell me," I prodded, shooting the shot the bartender slid me.

"Because you said you wanted to keep things professional. I'm trying to do what you asked. Ever since the kiss, I haven't been able to stop thinking about you and what I want to do to you," he confessed, knocking back a shot of his own.

And there's the truth.

"So you're ignoring me because you're attracted to me?"

"I find you breathtaking. You've come out of your shell so much lately, and it's welcoming to see. Your intelligence and kindness are dumbfounding, and I am completely enamored with you."

Wow.

I was stunned. We sat there in silence, our gaze locked and unbreaking. I found us to be at an impasse. We were damned if we did and damned if we didn't. I wasn't exactly itching to be seen as the girl with her boss, especially when I worked so hard to be seen as someone who stood on my own two feet. The truth was that he made me feel safe and comfortable to be who I was.

"So… where does that leave us?"

He took a deep breath and shifted his weight in his seat, facing me fully. Damon's hand touched the top of my thigh as our eyes interlocked.

I could feel myself starting to sweat. He made me nervous, giddy even. It was a crazy feeling, especially when it surfaced after knowing someone for most of my life.

I deserve happiness. I deserve to choose what I want.

"I want you," I whispered, scanning the bar for anyone who might be listening.

"Let's go." Damon took my hand in his, threw a twenty-dollar bill down for a tip, and pulled me out of there.

When we stepped into the cold night air, my arms began to goosebump as Damon pushed me up against the side of the building.

Fuck.

"It's been torture keeping my hands off you." His mouth closed the distance between us, claiming mine as our tongues tangled in a needing mess.

His hands wandered my body, landing on my ass as he cupped them, lifting me against the wall.

"Not. here," I said in between kisses.

I didn't want to risk a coworker seeing us. That would open up a lot of questions that I didn't feel ready or prepared to answer just yet.

"Where? My place or yours?"

"Neither. I want this… I do. But I don't want to rush it either." My heart rate slowed, allowing me to take a full breath.

A disappointed look flitted across his face. I couldn't blame him in the slightest. It was hard for me to say, but I knew it wasn't right for us yet. It was too important to screw this up, especially because it was him. It was Damon.

"Don't worry about it. I get it, Erin, I do. I would like to spend time with you, though. What do you say we go back to mine for a movie? That'll help us avoid any awkward questions from your parents or Ellison." A smile appeared on his face, and I felt myself give in.

"That sounds like a plan. Should I change out of this? Something more comfortable?" I gestured to my bar clothes.

"Only if you want. I have some clothes you can borrow if you're open to that, too."

Damon's shirt. That wasn't a bad idea.

He walked me to my car as he glanced around. His eyes were alert and fixed on scanning the area.

The part of him must be second nature by now. I'm sure the Navy drilled it into him.

"Everything look okay there, sir?" I joked.

He snapped out of it, laughing alongside me.

"Sorry, it's the murders. I feel like I'm on high alert all the time now. Here, you get in safe, and I'll follow you back to my house." Damon offered me his hand, helping me into my car as she shut the door behind me.

The drive was silent, as I opted to keep the radio off. Choosing to be alone in my thoughts was something I didn't always strive for. Right in this very moment, though, I was happy. I was hopeful.

Beep. Beep.

Damon honked behind me and signaled for me to pull over to the side of the road. As I did, I noticed all the lights a couple hundred feet ahead. In the glow of the lights, I could see a string of police cars and an ambulance.

Oh no.

"What's going on?" I asked Damon, who was all business and brusque.

"No idea. I wanted to check it out."

My heart tightened as I observed a barrage of people working in a frenzy, scurrying around like the mice in Cinderella. Something was going on, that was for sure. And it wasn't good.

We silently watched as the EMTs loaded someone onto the stretcher, covering them lightly with the sheet, and into the ambulance. As they drove away, they kept the sirens and lights off.

That only meant one thing. The person in it didn't need emergency services or medical assistance.

They were dead.

To confirm, they were likely murdered.

The killer wasn't slowing down or planning to stop anytime soon.

Chapter Ten

DAMON

Another murder and it was right under my nose. Once I realized that the person was dead, I sprinted over to the scene. Chief Dodds nodded my way as I approached, giving me the signal that he would talk to me later. We had kept each other in the loop throughout the investigation.

Erin followed closely behind, her eyes wide and terrified as she surveyed the scene. Officers were actively taping it off to keep the growing crowd at bay. I spotted Johnny in the distance, who appeared nervous, especially once his eyes landed on mine.

What are you really doing here?

As someone who served with me, I would never suspect Johnny of anything. When I knew him, he was a stand-up guy. Albeit, he could be a little cocky and irresponsible. He was never a killer. Yet here I was, years later, feeling uncomfortable and uneasy around him. There were just too many unanswered questions where he was concerned.

As he tucked the bottom of his shirt into his pants, I noticed a few dark red splotches.

Blood. I think.

His eyes trailed mine to my line of sight. He gave a pained look, then a recovered laugh. Johnny shook his head and then made a gun signal for "hunting." He liked to hunt in his spare time, but it wasn't something regularly done in this town.

What "job" was he really in town for?

What was he hiding that he couldn't share with me?

Why was he one of the first people on the scene?

Why is there something off about him?

Erin's hand slightly shook in mine, pulling me out of my thoughts and tossing me into the present time.

"Hey, Damon. It isn't good, man," Chief Dodds said, shaking my free hand as his gaze landed on Erin.

He doesn't want to share anything with her here.

"Can you give me a quick moment?" I asked Erin, patting her hand as I stepped to the side to ask the chief for more information.

"What's going on?"

"We received a call about an object spotted. Once officers arrived on the scene, they realized that it was another body. Our initial estimate puts the time of death around three to four hours ago. That's about all I can share right now. I know we have a little understanding, the two of us. However, I do have to keep the investigation solid."

Another body. They just keep coming.

"Thanks. I'll go home and compile everything I have. They can't keep getting away with it. They won't," I promised him.

It wasn't only a promise to him, but to myself, my family, my friends… to Erin.

"Erin, let's go." I pulled her arm as we made our way back to the cars.

I wanted nothing more than just to go home, turn on a movie, and forget about the fact that some sociopath was picking off innocent people in our town one by one. I couldn't, though. Not in good conscience.

"I can't believe it. It doesn't even feel safe to go out anymore. Did you want to reschedule our impromptu movie night? I would completely understand."

"No, no, I want to spend time with you. Come over still. I have something I want to show you. If you like, we can still watch a movie."

She smiled and nodded as she got into her car and pulled toward my house.

As I drove home, I ran through the facts of the case in my head. Fact number one—we knew that the kills had almost nothing in common besides the cause of death and the same killer. That, we were sure of. Number two—they were moving at a rapid rate. The biggest takeaway for me is that they're getting sloppy. The first murders took place in the home, out of the public eye. This body was left on the side of the road, strangled as well. Was the murder done there? Or was it dragged there? I almost hoped for the latter, knowing they likely left a great deal of evidence behind.

Leaving someone on the side of the road like that was equivalent to leaving a sign that said, "I'm right here. Please catch me."

And yet, I still had no leads. The police didn't have any leads. Andrew was a possibility, but I didn't have anything on him yet other than that he made Erin suspicious. Johnny… could I even qualify him as a suspect?

Erin was sitting on my porch as I pulled into the driveway. Her legs were crossed, and her hair was blowing in the breeze. Her face was screwed up, clearly lost in thought as she looked to the side.

"Been here long?" I closed the car door behind me.

"Me? Oh, for ages. You sure know how to keep a girl waiting," she joked, but it lacked humor. She was putting on a front.

We emerged into the house, and I started to switch on the lights. Ensuring the deadbolt was latched behind me, I offered her something to drink.

"Water. I think I need to sober up," she said.

"Sounds good. Two waters coming right up. Hungry?"

"No, thanks, Damon. I love what you've done with everything here. It's a major facelift since your parents owned it," she complimented, admiring the home.

It was true. I hated to toot my own horn, but I was all about changing up the dated space to fit my needs for the home. It ended up turning out better than I could have ever imagined.

"I appreciate that. However, you may have to tell Chip and Joanna Gaines about that. I watched a lot of Fixer-Upper before I started any renovations for the house. Here you go." I passed her the water.

"What do you think about the latest murder? Weird, right?" I eyed Erin curiously.

"To be honest, it scares the living daylights out of me. But you know what I was thinking? Doing it in public or changing the pattern is unhinged, isn't it?"

My thoughts exactly.

"I don't have any stand-out suspects right now, though. It's frustrating."

But Johnny is looking more and more suspicious.

"What about that guy, Andrew? New to town, shady, unsettling?" she offered.

Maybe.

"I want to show you something," I blurted out after some time had passed.

"Sure. What is it?" Erin pushed to stand.

"Follow me." I gestured to me, and Erin quickly did. I had been conducting my own research for a while, and I finally felt ready to share it with another person besides the chief.

"Woah. What is this stuff?"

My hands found the light switch in the bedroom as I pointed out all my research. I had pinned every clue and tip to the corkboard that took up most of the wall of my small guest bedroom. Her jaw hung open, taking in everything all at once. I don't think I had ever seen Erin speechless; it was something to witness.

"My vendetta, I suppose. I have been looking into the truth about the murders since they happened. This can't happen here, not to the people who have lived in and loved this town their whole lives. It doesn't seem fair." I sat down.

She joined me, grabbing my hand in hers. Her face had a solemn and pitiful look to it.

"I had no idea about any of this. I have so many questions! Does Ellison know? Do you have any suspects?"

"He doesn't. I haven't told anyone. Especially not my sister, so please don't mention anything to her. As for suspects… I'm not doing too great. I've looked at people new to town since they started, but besides you, I haven't found anything."

"What about Andrew?" Erin tapped her chin thoughtfully.

"I haven't found much, but I wanted to do a deeper dive. That's on tonight's agenda. Are you up for a long night?" I offered her a bottle of water from the table.

"Oh, yeah."

During the course of note-taking, profile building,

report reading, and more, we found ourselves laughing and then drifting off to sleep. When I woke in the middle of the night, I had Andrew's information stuck in my mind. Erin was sleeping peacefully, sprawled on the chaise lounge chair, her hair splayed wildly.

I got back to work. According to the report, he was a true crime junkie who had been featured in several news stories over the years. It was mostly for his scattered eyewitness reports, which had later been proven to be false. He was somewhat of a sensationalist and a little off his rocker.

Now, he was here for no reason other than that he wanted some of the limelight for the murders. My professional opinion? He was harmless, but I did know better than to judge a book by its cover.

Erin had been busy at work creating a profile workup for the killer. It was her first time doing so in a criminal sense format, so she had erased and rewritten her thoughts all night. She refused to show it to me until she could ensure it was done to her standards.

From what I had seen, it looked done. I would respect her wishes, though.

Gosh, she looks breathtaking when she's asleep.

Her phone buzzed with a message from her mom.

"Uh-oh, your mom is freaking out." I shook Erin awake.

Half-asleep, she rolled her eyes and typed a reply.

"Come to the guest room. You don't want to sleep on the chaise; trust me. It will kill your back." I helped Erin stand, guiding her to the room.

She collapsed on the bed in exhaustion as I covered her with a thick blanket. My body felt wiped out, the same as her, and I dragged into my own bed as I slipped into sleep.

"Rise and shine…" I opened my eyes to find Erin holding a plate of bacon, eggs, and toast.

Did she cook this? In my kitchen?

"Yes, I know what you're thinking. Yes, I cooked. I'm a good house guest, if anything. I appreciate you letting me crash here. I was too wiped to make it back over there last night." She slid the tray onto my lap, sitting by my feet.

She had changed out of her outfit from the night before and donned one of my t-shirts and basketball shorts.

"I appreciate it, although you didn't have to. It was no trouble at all. In fact, you're the one I should thank. I think I hit a breakthrough last night."

"Oh, yeah. What was that?"

"I'm not convinced that Andrew did it. I think he's just someone here to take advantage of the situation. He wants to bring fame to himself by using our town and our tragedy."

"So, who do we look into next?"

"I hate to say it… but Johnny. He's new to town, and he's being very vague and suspicious. He's a good friend of mine, but he's not an idiot. If he's involved in some way, he won't be easily caught. He also is smart."

Johnny is a good guy, and he was always noble and good-natured. But it was clear that the violence we experienced in our line of work didn't affect him the way it had the rest of us. When faced with having to commit violent acts, he was at peace with it. He seemingly *enjoyed* it. That was the one thing about him that never quite sat right with me.

"I want to help," she crossed her arms.

"I thought you were helping."

"No, I mean for real. I want to be involved with the investigation. I can offer my profiling and behavioral assessment skills. I know this town pretty well, too." She playfully punched my shoulder.

"Deal."

"You enjoy your breakfast. I should get back to the house. My mom has been on my case, and this won't be an easy one to explain away." She leaned across me, planted a kiss on my cheek, and then she was off.

I heard the front door close as I started to enjoy the food. She was a damn good cook. My mealtime was interrupted by an incoming phone call.

From Johnny.

"Hey, man."

"Hi, Damon. Look, I wanted to call because I know you saw me last night… at the crime scene. I didn't get a chance to explain why I was there, so I wanted to call you." His voice sounded nervous.

"What? You don't need to explain yourself. We all flock to stuff like that here because it's so rare. Well, it was. Maybe it's wearing off on you. How's your trip going? Is the job done?"

"No, the job is still ongoing. But the trip was good. I wish I could spend a little more time catching up with you, brother. Let's plan a time this week, yeah?"

"Sure thing, Johnny. See you then." I clicked the phone, hanging up the call.

Yeah, we will have to stick to that. I have to see him in person.

I just hoped my gut feeling was wrong and that my friend was who I had always thought he was.

Hopefully.

Chapter Eleven

ERIN

I was going to help Damon find the killer. It wasn't exactly where I pictured myself while consuming textbooks from cover to cover throughout school. Yet here I was, feeling brave enough with Damon's influence to offer my insight into tracking down the person responsible for single-handedly terrorizing an entire town.

He made me feel brave, an emotion that was utterly unfamiliar to me. I wasn't exactly some scared little girl, but my entire life, I had been comfortable hanging on the sidelines, staying out of the line of fire.

The morning wrapped up quickly after we ate breakfast. I knew that I should head home soon before my mom had an aneurysm. She didn't like the idea of me not sleeping in my bed while all this was going on, although she softened at the idea of me being at Damon's house. They trusted him implicitly.

And so did I.

"Mom, I'm home!" I shut the door behind me.

"Thank goodness! You had me worried sick. Did you hear about the new murder? It's in plain sight now! Have people no shame? How was Damon's?" She held me at arm's length, examining me closely.

For what, I wasn't exactly sure. Ellison looked up from his morning paper and rolled his eyes, holding back a laugh.

Weird. Both of them.

"It was fine, mom. We had a ton of work to get done, that's all. I need a shower. I feel gross from not taking one last night. It's so humid out already." I started to jump up the stairs, taking them two by two.

"You're sure right. It's fixing to be a hot one today!" my dad shouted out of eyesight.

As the lather rinsed out of my hair, I ran through parts of the case that Damon shared with me. We had determined the killer lived in or near town since the murders all happened here. Also, each one had been restrained in some way and had dirt and splinters under their fingernails. Had they been locked in a basement?

"Erin! Get down here!" my parents screamed in unison.

My heart dropped as I wrapped myself in a robe, rapidly descending the stairs in an anxious flurry.

"What! What is it?"

"Latest update. Sit." My dad pointed to the television and patted the couch next to him.

"We are coming at you live with a new update on the serial killer case. As of this evening, police have added another body to the roster- Anna Williams, a thirty-year-old bank teller. They have no details other than that to release at this time but are issuing a town-wide lockdown. Besides necessary outings such as grocery, gas, work, and others, residents are to remain safely in their homes…"

The news anchor, Chelsea Song, rattled off more information.

My mouth gaped open in shock as I stared mindlessly at the TV set.

A lockdown?

Jesus. It was getting really bad. My phone started to ring upstairs, so I excused myself to get dressed and answer it.

"Hello?" I didn't bother looking at the caller ID.

"Hey, you. Did you see the news?" A velvet voice echoed through the earpiece.

Damon.

"I did. This is all so unbelievable. I guess they're scared. They're grasping at straws to keep any more murders from happening."

"It won't. This person is clearly desperate. Doing it on an open road? Leaving it out like that? They're getting sloppy."

He sounded so sure, and it gave me all the reason not to want to question it. He had much more experience than I did when it came to things like this. He had seen things, *lived* them. Everything I knew was from a textbook at this point.

"Well, since I can't go most anywhere right now, what do you say we hunker down and try and figure things out? I started to work on a killer profile."

There was silence on the other end of the phone, and I wondered if I was overstepping. We did have a great time last night, but what if I was moving too fast? It was entirely possible that being together two days in a row was already too much.

"Of course. We can order pizza. I think that may be lockdown-approved, right?" I could hear his smile through the phone.

"Worth a shot. I'll be over in an hour or two."

I quickly dressed. The murders were starting to weigh on me. When I first arrived, my attitude aligned more with the "don't let 'em keep you down" approach. It was becoming increasingly harder and harder to do so with each death that came. These were people. They have lives, families, and jobs. I owed it to myself and my family to muster up any knowledge I had to help catch the killer… in the best way I could.

After all, I had scored at the top of my class during the profile modules. I was confident I could easily create a profile connected to the killer's identity. Damon was a big help as well. I knew we could do it. It would just take some time.

"Hey, Mom?" I popped my head around the corner of the upper hallway.

"Yes, dear?" She exited her bedroom, carrying a folded stack of freshly laundered towels.

I embraced her in a tight squeeze as she handed them to me.

"It'll all be okay, you know that, right?"

"I know. I just want you safe."

"I am. I was going to pop back over to Damon's. I wanted to give you a heads up." I released her as I stepped back to grab my purse.

"What's going on with you two, seriously?"

"Honestly? I like him. He's an amazing guy. I don't know if we'll ever be anything more than friends, though. Time will tell… truth." I held my hand up, swearing my word.

"Well, you have my blessing… if that means anything. I've always admired him.

She turned on her heels and stalked off to the towel closet, fueled by purpose.

"Going somewhere? There's a lockdown, princess," Ellison reminded me as I reached for the front door handle.

"I know that. I'm going next door."

"More work? That's a lot of overtime. Such a shame I'm not getting any… *work*, I mean." He folded his arms across his chest.

Oh, God. Now my entire family thinks we're sleeping together.

"Please don't project your insecurities onto me again. I'm leaving now, goodbye. See you later."

The door was slamming behind me before he could get another word in.

He was absolutely infuriating sometimes. My brother always had a penchant for being able to get under my skin in ways that nobody else has. Call it sibling rivalry or whatever. He was always the golden boy growing up—good grades, star athlete, jock… you name it. If there was something to be done, you better believe that Ellison could accomplish it with a smile on his face and swarms of girls in his wake.

I was the scholar, the bookworm. My parents were always proud of me, and that was a positive thing. But when it came to popularity, I didn't even measure up. Ellison and I were not even on the same scale.

To have him lecturing me felt uncomfortable, to say the least. I didn't deserve it and didn't feel like tolerating it. I was sure to go crazy if I was stuck in the same house as him forever. I loved my brother immensely, but space was good sometimes.

I promised myself that once the killer was found and everything was safe, I would find my own place.

"Hey, you." Damon swung the door open, wearing a black fitted t-shirt and jeans.

Wow. He is completely alluring.

"Hi, should we get to work?" I said, trying to swallow my conflicting emotions.

On the one hand, I was excited to see him. On the other, I was angry at my brother. Finally, I was feeling frustrated with the lockdown.

"Everything okay with you? You seem off." Damon's brows furrowed.

"It's Ellison. He's just irritating sometimes. You know how siblings can be," a smile spread across my lips.

I leaned back on the couch. My head had started pounding.

I had never felt so much tension between myself and a man. There were men here and there in college. Lord knows I wasn't a nun. But there was something different about Damon. The air was charged between us. A fire burned within me whenever he was around, and it was that much brighter the closer we were.

Suddenly, he closed the distance between us, cupping my face in his hands. His gaze was smoldering, packed full of lust.

"You're something special, Erin. It's completely bewildering to me," he confessed.

Woah. Is it cliche to say ditto?

"I could say the same thing. I'm in awe of you." My hand found his thigh, giving it a gentle squeeze.

Damon slowly leaned in, his lips hovering an inch or two above mine as if waiting for confirmation from me. My other hand found his cheek, pulling him in.

Our lips crashed into each other. The kiss wasn't as aggressive and needy as it was earlier. It was slow, passionate. Our lips moved without hurry as our tongues twisted and tangled with each other, hands wandering each other's bodies.

My lower half felt like it was on fire, heat spreading

through my veins as the pleasure began to build. His touch was electric, and I was putty.

"Sorry, I wanted to do that since you walked in the door," Damon apologized as he pulled from this kiss.

No, I need more.

His hands searched the couch for the remote, and I knew the moment was over. I wanted to take it slow, but every moment I spent with him made it challenging.

"Don't apologize." I winked.

"I know we said we would work, but it's the weekend. Let's take a little break and watch a movie. It's rare that I have someone to do things like this with. My parents have their own life, and my sister has her hands full as it is. So what do you say?" He smiled at me.

And he's choosing to do it with me.

"Absolutely. You pick." I snuggled into his side.

To my surprise, he chose a romantic comedy. I was expecting something like *John Wick* or *The Terminator*. It seemed as if he was thinking about what I was would prefer. So *Love Actually* it was.

We sat happily as we watched the movie, laughing as we did.

The only thing that disturbed us was the banging at the door.

Damn it.

Chapter Twelve

DAMON

Bang. Bang. Bang.

Erin's head shot straight up, the warmth of her body lingering on mine.

Who the hell is that?

"Give me a second." I paused the movie as I stomped off to the front door.

Johnny.

Moving from the peephole, I cracked the door. He looked wrecked. Johnny's eyes were bloodshot, and he had scratch marks on his hand.

"What's going on, man?"

"I have to talk to you." He pushed inside.

Out of the corner of my eye, Erin crouched down on the side of the couch, staying out of sight. She didn't want to be seen by him, and I felt grateful that she chose to do that.

Johnny wasn't acting like himself, and I wasn't sure if I

trusted him or not. It was better to be safe than sorry, especially when he looked like this.

"I hate to barge in, but I don't have anyone else to talk to her. You're my only friend, man."

"So, talk to me. You look like you've been through hell."

We both took a seat at the kitchen counter as I pushed a glass of ice water towards him.

"Thanks." He knocked the entire glass back in three large gulps.

What the fuck.

"I'm not proud of myself, Damon. When I served, I felt like a hero. Now, I can't even look at myself in the mirror. I feel disgusted with myself."

"What do you mean? You are a hero, man. You have always been one of the most stand-up guys I know."

He guffawed as he shook his head slightly.

"Believe me, I'm nobody to look up to." He rubbed his temples.

"So tell me what's going on. How can I help you?"

"You can't. I don't think anybody can. I'm in too deep. I owe too much."

"Whatever it is, I'm here for you. I can't keep seeing you like this. You have a child that needs you, and I refuse to let you fall any deeper into this hole that you've found yourself in."

He shook his head, then put it in his hands. As he opened his mouth to speak, the phone rang.

I reached for my cell phone, as did he, but neither was ringing.

Fuck.

"Who's phone is that? Who's here?" he accused, already on his feet.

"Nobody, man. I think Erin left her phone here from earlier."

"Why are you lying to me? Where is she?" He started frantically looking around.

I glanced over to the couch, but Erin was gone.

Smart girl.

"Stop it! You need to get a handle on yourself."

"Whatever. I'm out of here. This was a mistake." He stormed off towards the door, slamming it behind him.

The wall shook in his wake, and I couldn't help but shake my head. I have never seen Johnny act anything other than level-headed and calm. This was a new side to the friend that I knew and loved. Something was going on with him, and seeing how far he had fallen was terrifying. I was at a loss for what to do for him. He made it pretty clear that he didn't want to divulge anything to me.

I want to help him.

"I assume it's safe to come out." Erin emerged from the bedroom.

"Yes, it is. I'm so sorry about that. I don't know what's gotten into him." I patted the couch next to me.

"Can I put in my two cents? And I don't want you to get upset." She slid onto the seat beside me.

"Of course you can. I welcome your opinion."

"Have you considered that he might have something to do with the murders? I mean, it's undeniable on my end. He showed up right around the time they started. He's acting out of character, he said he's doing a "job," and he's apparently disgusted with himself. To me, it reads pretty black and white. Some of the evidence you showed me indicated someone unhinged, and I had a lightbulb moment last night. The person who's committing the crimes is a violent person—and this is the part where I don't want you to be offended—he had a job that one could consider very violent. In my limited time back, I don't see any other standout suspects. I don't know. Maybe I'm grasping at straws here."

I considered it. But no, he can't be.

"No way. He's an upstanding guy. Whatever he's going through, he would never resort to murder. It's got to be something else."

Did I believe that?

"Alright, I trust your judgment. I wonder what is going on, though. He seemed so frantic."

My stomach grumbled in protest. The only meal I had so far was the breakfast she cooked for me.

"I know. But hey, let's not let it ruin our evening. Steak? I can cook."

"Sounds good," she leaned back, and I planted a chaste kiss on her forehead, heading to the kitchen.

Rolling my sleeves up, I began to take out all the ingredients, one by one. As I threw the steaks onto the pan to lightly sear, I turned up the radio and grabbed Erin's hand, pulling her to her feet.

"What are you doing?" she laughed in protest.

"Dancing, c'mon." I spun her around.

Smooth jazz played through the house as we rocked back and forth, throwing a spin in every few minutes.

"That's my foot." I half-growled, half-chuckled.

"Sorry, I'm not the best dancer." Erin tried to pull away, but my arms tightened.

You're not going anywhere, sweetheart.
Beep. Beep. Beep.

The smoke alarm was going haywire. I had forgotten about the steaks. I let go of Erin and sprinted to the kitchen, removing them from the heat. They were slightly charred on one side.

Well, slow cooker it was then. Quickly chopping the

steak into pieces and carefully removing the burnt ends, I tossed everything inside the crockpot and poured in some beef broth, setting it on high for two hours.

"I hope you're not too hungry, because this is going to take a few hours."

"Not at all. That gives us time to work on finding the killer," she said as she reentered the room holding some paperwork.

"Let's do this." I sat down at the dining table, making room.

We used plain sheets of paper to map out a timeline and theories for the murders. We had different opinions on some of them, and so we wanted to compare and contrast.

"We know it's someone who lives here. It has to be. Why else would someone come from out of town only to kill residents one by one? And we know they are holding the victims somewhere—maybe where they kill them."

"And the latest kill, it was done in plain sight. The person isn't calming down with each kill. They're only getting more and more amped up. It's fueling them, but it's also unraveling them."

I do agree with that. It's pretty brazen to leave the body in the road like that. Granted, it wasn't a popular area, so the traffic wasn't too heavy.

"It sounds about time for a break. Let me check on the food." I stood, jogging to the kitchen.

Sure enough, the meat was tender and the vegetables soft. When I turned, she was already seated at the dining table, laying a napkin on her lap.

God, she looks beautiful.

"Here you go, the Damon special," I joked, setting the food in front of her.

Her eyes widened as she smelled the food.

"This looks amazing. Your recipe, huh?"

"The one and only. I like to make do with what I have. It's a honed skill."

We made our way through our plates. After we finished, Erin leaned back and jokingly patted her stomach.

"I have a full-on food baby."

"Same here. Want to continue the break and watch something?"

It was so nice to have someone with me to just relax and hang out with. Sure, I had friends. I had family. But it was lonely living alone sometimes. I had girlfriends over the years, but it was never anything serious. None of them had met my family, and none stayed for very long. They just weren't good fits.

"Hello?" Erin answered the phone, but I hadn't even heard it ringing.

"Yes, I am. How are you? Aw, that's good. Yeah, I miss you too. I'll have to come over soon. How's Jonas?"

She's talking to my sister.

"Really? That makes me happy. Alright, Cara. I love you, bye." She hung up.

"How does it go with my baby sister?" I sat back down.

"Good… good. I know she and Jonas had a few off days, but he got a promotion at work, and she says they're doing better. The kids are good, too."

"Did you tell her you were over here?" I inquired, not holding her gaze.

"No… was I supposed to?" Her eyebrow raised.

"I guess not. Do you think she would be upset? That we were hanging out?"

And there it was. The question that had been at the back of my mind but I was avoiding. It scared me in more ways than one.

If I was worried about Cara's reaction to me hanging out with Erin, then I was in deep. I had feelings for her, and I cared about what my family and the people around me would think. Would they support me? The fact that Ellison did seem a little wary of the two of us had made me apprehensive about everyone else's feelings. It was clear that we liked each other.

I also didn't want to get our families involved, only for it not to work out. Even though it felt different than any other relationship I had possibly ever had, there was a lot to risk. There were friendships and families, and it felt selfish to only think about my wants and desires… as strong as they were.

"What? Why would she be? Did she say something?"

"No, not at all. I just… I really like you. I like this—us hanging out, spending time together. It's the highlight of my day, quite honestly."

She took a sharp inhale of breath. Her hand found mine on the table and gave it a gentle, reassuring squeeze. Erin's eyes met mine in an intense gaze, and it was clear. She felt the same.

"I feel the same way. I want you, Damon. I don't think anyone in our families would feel opposed to it. Even if they did, it doesn't matter to me. My own happiness is important, too, and you make me happy. You make me feel safe in a time when the outside world is incredibly unsafe."

Oh my god.

I pulled her in tight and squeezed her against me. She kissed my cheek, then slowly moved down, releasing me from the hug.

What is she doing?

And then she was backing up towards the counter, pulling herself up quickly. I stepped forward as her eyes scanned up and down my body hungrily. Our lips collided, and her hands fumbled and tore at my clothes.

I need to taste her.

Dropping down, I slowly lifted her dress as her beautiful green eyes met mine for confirmation. She nodded breathlessly as she gripped my hair. Sliding the seam of her red lace panties to the side, my tongue explored her as my thumb focused on her swollen clit.

She was moaning, her head moving up and down as she gripped my hair and simultaneously steadied herself on the counter. It was clear Erin was building quickly. My hands gripped her thighs, securing her into place as I brought her to the edge. Erin came undone as she let out a string of curses and screams.

She sat up, wiping a bead of sweat from her forehead as a smile slowly spread. I had no idea she ever had that in her.

"You are incredible," she giggled.

"And you… *taste* incredible," I said as I kissed her and pulled her close.

I would never get enough of this woman.

Chapter Thirteen

ERIN

The lockdown had lifted. The police soon realized they couldn't keep people isolated in their homes without some kind of pushback. Of course, some people welcomed it, like my mother. They were the people who were keeping close to the house anyway.

On the other hand, I had been going stir-crazy. I was ready for the weekend.

I had been spending every night at Damon's house, unwinding and working hard to assemble pieces of the case. The most daunting task was putting together a profile for the killer, which was nearly done.

With all this going on, my mind remained on Damon and the dangerous things he could do with his tongue.

"What, are you living together now?" Ellison prompted as I poured myself a cup of coffee.

"No, were not. Does it truly bug you that we've been hanging out? You like Damon."

"That's not what bugs me. It's that you're not being honest about it. You have feelings for him. Admit it."

"Alright. I have feelings for him. We have feelings for each other. Neither of us expected it, but it's something we're both okay with. I hope you'll be supportive and understanding, but if you're not, that's on you. I love you. But if you can't respect my choices, then that's your problem and your problem only," I confessed, anger building with my brother.

He stood silently for a moment, almost as if processing my confession, before finally speaking.

"That's all I wanted to hear. If you're happy, then I'm happy." Ellison pulled me in for a hug.

Thank God.

"I heard that," my mom chuckled, passing by with a trash bag.

She winked at me as she rounded the corner, and my heart soared at the acceptance of my family. During the lockdown, there had been no murders. I hadn't received any text messages, and the police were still at a standstill. There was nothing connecting the victims, meaning they were chosen at random, which made it even harder to narrow down the killer.

"Well, I'm off to work. Love you all," I shouted, closing the door behind me.

I had a little time before work, so I wanted to stop at the bakery on the way in. Damon loved the blueberry muffins there, so it would be nice to surprise him. I noted that his car was already gone when I left, so he must have gone into work early.

The early bird gets the worm, as Damon so annoyingly said.

My hair was not working well for me today and was still sitting in a mess atop my head. I quickly ran a brush through it as I let my car warm up, then pulled it into a neat bun.

Oldies from the 90s played on the radio as I parked in the bakery parking lot. It was quite crowded, unlike how empty it had been during the lockdown.

How refreshing.

Some people felt suffocated during the temporary lockdown, so they were going out even more than before. I considered that a minor win. Living in fear wasn't good for anyone.

"Hi, what can I get you?"

"I'm going to get two blueberry muffins, please."

She was an older woman with graying hair, and it just made me think about the poor woman who I had seen only the week prior who was murdered. Life could be gone in an instant, and the thought was sobering.

"Here, thank you." I handed her my money, and she passed two pastry bags over to me.

The line behind me was starting to go out the door.

I should probably get some napkins.

"Are those any good?" a voice behind me spoke.

Turning, I tried to keep the smile on my face from vanishing.

Andrew.

"They're delicious. It looks like your spot is all packed. How have you been?"

He was still wearing the hoodie pulled up close to his face. It didn't soften his look at all, and only made him look more suspicious.

"It's great to see everyone back out and about. It's no fun when everyone's tucked in the house. I was going to ask —do you like jazz?" He looked me up and down, a strange smile on his face.

"I'm not the biggest fan. Why do you ask?"

"I have two tickets for the jazz concert over in Pensington. I thought you might like to go with me."

"Oh, that's so sweet of you. I'm seeing someone right now, but thank you for considering me. " I smiled and plucked a few napkins from the dispenser.

"Well, he's a lucky guy. Bye," Andrew stalked off, his hands balled at his side.

What the hell is that all about?

"I don't know why he would want to invite me. We barely know each other. Also, why would he invite me to a concert over an hour's drive away? I don't know. It just made me uncomfortable," I told Damon in his office shortly after I arrived at work.

"How did he seem when you told him no?" He crossed his arms over his chest.

"He was angry. You could tell."

"I did look into him. He had one restraining order from an ex-girlfriend when he lived in Florida, but other than that, he was pretty squeaky clean. Stay away from him, though." He rubbed my arm comfortingly.

"Yeah, you're right. Do you know why he had the restraining order against him?"

"Stalking his ex-girlfriend and some minor threats."

That's just great. One of my only suitors besides Damon in over a year, and he's a suspicious stalker.

"Yikes. I'm going to get started on some work, but I wanted to update you. Have a good day." I leaned to kiss him, and his hands grabbed my waist and pulled me in tight for more.

His tongue pushed its way into my mouth, and we lost ourselves in the moment as our tongues tangled in a passionate tango before a knock at the door broke the kiss.

"Come in," Damon coughed, straightening his tie.

I waved at him as I stepped around Charles, who gave me a knowing side-eye.

Taking a seat at my desk, I was suddenly overwhelmed by everything going on. According to Damon, he was in close contact with the police on updates involving the case. They had made it clear that they had a few suspects, but nothing panned out. Additional resources were allocated, including reviewing video footage from any business near the murders to track comings and goings. Unfortunately, most of the apartments and homes were in areas away from the town businesses and out of camera view.

It seemed like there was no progress. I wanted to walk down the street and not have the urge to look over my shoulder. I wouldn't keep myself locked away, but I didn't feel one hundred percent safe.

My phone started to ring.

"Hello, this is Erin Summers."

"Erin, hi. It's Jordan… Nash. I'm the principal at—"

"At the elementary school, I remember. How are you?"

"I'm doing well, thank you. I know I initially said you were too good for this job, which I still firmly believe. Unfortunately, we have still yet to fill the position, so I thought I would reach out and see if you were open to taking it," he said all in one breath.

"Wow, I appreciate you reaching back out. I did take another position, however." I tapped my knuckles on my desk.

"That's unfortunate to hear, but I'm not surprised. That brings me to my next order of business…"

"Yes?" I sat up straighter in my seat.

"I was wondering if you were free for some drinks sometime."

Woah, two for two today. I'm on a roll. But I'm taken, unofficially.

"Wow, that's very sweet. I am seeing someone at the moment as well. I'm sorry."

There was a cough and a knock on the open door. Damon was standing there, leaning against the doorframe, looking quite amused.

"I understand. Well, if anything changes, you have my number. Bye, Erin."

"Bye," I said, but he had already hung up.

As I set the phone down, Damon made his way over to me.

"So many suitors in one day. I'm thinking I have to step my game up." He chuckled.

I rolled my eyes.

"It's not funny. Rejection is never fun, and I feel horrible doing that to someone."

"I know, I get it. Hey, I was just stopping in to tell you to come by tonight. I wanted to talk to you about something."

"I'm by almost every night, anyways. What's going on?" My mind buzzed with possibilities.

"Just stop by. Alright, I have to get back. See you," and he was gone.

It made me extremely nervous. Maybe he had decided that this was too much for him. Or that he didn't want to be in a relationship after all… not that we were in anything official.

I only had a few hours of work left, but I was wracked with anxiety.

As I punched out later, I saw Charles was already gone for the evening. The door to Damon's office was open, and there was no sight of him either.

The drive to his house had my palms sweating. I had switched the AC on and off about fifteen times. I was either too hot or cold, but I was undoubtedly anxious.

"Hey, you." He swung the door open before I could even knock.

I slowly climbed the front steps, a small smile on my face.

"Why do you look so nervous?" he asked as he closed the door behind me.

"Oh, I don't know. Maybe it's because you told me we needed to talk, and then left me to revel in a million possibilities. So tell me."

The corner of his lip turned into a smirk as Damon closed the distance between us. His hands found mine, and he looked into my eyes.

"You are the most frustrating, wonderful, stubborn woman I have ever met."

"Okay…" I mumbled.

"And I don't know how I've lived this long without you. You've always been around. Since you came back, I've seen a different side of you. This is incredibly cheesy, but I want to make things official, *this* official." He motioned between the two of us.

"Damon Clark… are you asking me to be your girlfriend? At your ripe old age?" I giggled.

"Why, yes, I think I am. So, what'll it be?"

"Of course. It's not even a question."

He picked me up, spinning me around as he kissed my cheeks, forehead, and lips.

This is heaven.

"Now, you may have noticed I rushed out of work today. It was so I could get this together…" He stepped back, motioning to the romantic display behind him.

The floor was covered in rose petals, and on the counter were two small gift bags and a pizza from our local spot.

"You're wonderful."

His phone rang, and he squinted as he read the caller's name.

"Ellison, what's going on? Yes… she's here, why? Are you serious? Okay. I'll tell her. How've you been, man? I haven't seen much of you at work or otherwise. I know, work's been crazy. Okay, bye."

He hung up the phone.

"My brother? What did he say?"

"He wanted to make sure you were safe. There was a break-in at Joe's Coffee Shop."

Chapter Fourteen

DAMON

We were together, officially. It became increasingly clear to me in the days that followed our first kiss that I wanted to be with her.

I was old enough to know what I wanted. I wanted her. I don't think I have ever been surer of anything in my life. She said yes, and my heart soared. It all came crashing down when I received a call from Ellison, who said there was a break-in at the local coffee shop.

I couldn't be sure that it was related to the murders, but we usually had such a low crime rate that it seemed unlikely to be anything else. However, I couldn't for the life of me figure out why they would break into the coffee shop. Ellison wasn't sure what they had taken, but he had seen it on the news. They caught footage of the person as they broke in from behind. They were wearing a black hoodie with their face hidden from the camera.

News reporters hadn't confirmed the theory, but

Ellison told me he thought it was a man. He agreed to text me video footage. Erin left shortly after the call to spend some time at her house. Her mother ramped up in worry when something like this happened. She jumped into mama bear mode and wanted to protect them fiercely, even though they were adults. My parents were also worried, but they knew I could protect myself. They hardly worried about Cara as she had Jonas in the house.

There was nothing I could do at the moment about the break-in. Erin was safe at home, and I had something on my mind that I needed to do something about as soon as possible. Knowing where Johnny was, I took it upon myself to pay him a visit. My friend was hurting, and if I didn't do anything to help him or figure out what was going on, then I couldn't live with myself.

That's not the kind of person I am.

"Open up, Johnny. I know you're in there, man." I banged on his door.

Trash sat in large piles scattered loosely around his trailer, mostly empty beer cans.

Jesus, Johnny.

"Go away, Damon." He shouted from inside. The blinds cracked slightly.

You asked for this.

I leveled my foot as I kicked in the door, forcing the wood to splinter.

"What are you doing, man?! That's my door!" Johnny protested.

"I'll buy you a new one. We need to talk."

"No, we don't. I said all I wanted to say earlier. But I can't say any more, man."

"You're in a bad place, and you're my friend. I'm here for you. Is it alcohol? Drugs? You can be honest with me," I said as I sat on his worn-down couch.

"Did you know that my ex-wife is trying to get full custody of our daughter?" He took a swig out of an old bottle.

"I didn't. Is that what's upsetting you? I'm sorry. Custody stuff is tough."

"Losing my job right around that time was just the icing on the cake. You know, I had to start taking odd jobs here and there to avoid being homeless."

"I'm so sorry, Johnny. I wish you would have reached out. I would have been there for you. You could've come to work with me," I said, feeling sad for my friend.

"Yeah? The offer still apply? Me and you, back together in the workplace?" He chuckled, but his laugh lacked humor.

"Not in this state. You sober up, then absolutely. I think we should get you help, man."

"No. I think it's time you go. Please."

He stood up straight, looking down at me angrily as I sat. There was no use talking to him in his inebriated state. He would only get more and more aggressive and irrational. I gave him a sympathetic half-smile as I turned and walked out quickly.

His car was parked off to the side behind a tree. I half-expected him to come out fuming after me, but he didn't. Instead, I could hear music being turned up inside. Feeling the door handle of the driver's seat, it opened immediately.

Unlocked.

Wanting to work quickly, I scrambled in and began to look around for something… *anything* that would give me insight into the trouble that he was in.

Same as his home, there was a lot of trash and empty alcohol containers. I found a stack of paperwork, though, that looked like receipts for electronic payments made to Johnny. The memo line only read "Pictures."

I pulled open the glovebox to find a large envelope. It was filled with four-by-six photos.

Oh my gosh.

They were photos of women, all taken without their knowledge. Some were undressing, and some were outside—by a pool, gardening, and other things.

What the hell is this, Johnny?

I pulled out my phone and took pictures of the envelopes and the paperwork. Jumping out of the car, I ran to mine and took off before he noticed. A major ethical dilemma now hung over my head. He was my friend, someone I fought alongside and who I trusted wholeheartedly. But he had changed—he was no longer the same person. The Johnny I knew was not capable of something like this.

However, if I turned him in, I ran the risk of compromising him ever getting custody of his daughter. He would likely do some form of jail time. It was a big decision, and funnily enough, Erin was the only person I wanted to talk about it with. I texted her to meet me at my house in fifteen minutes. She would help me clear my head and figure out what to do, because I was at a loss.

As I parked the car, Erin was sitting on my porch looking worried. Her legs were crossed and brows furrowed in angst.

"Hey, you," I sighed.

Seeing her was like coming up for air. Her smile made my problems vanish, or at the very least, gave me someone I could vent about them to. I was never someone who liked to sit and talk about my feelings at length. In my previous job, keeping your emotions at bay was an asset. With Erin, I felt emotionally raw. She made me vulnerable, and I didn't hate it.

"Hi, handsome. You have me worried, what's going on?"

"Let's talk inside. It's a sensitive subject," I whispered, unlocking the front door.

We sat opposite each other on the couch while I cleared my throat, gathering the courage to tell her what I had found. It still felt pretty unbelievable to me, and saying it out loud to someone else felt like it would make it true.

"I think I figured out what Johnny is up to. I searched his car, and I found invoices. In the glove compartment, there were images he had taken."

Her eyes widened, "What kind of images?"

"They were all different. Some were taken of women undressing, some fully naked, and some were them at the store or something like that. But one thing was for certain with all of them—they were taken without their knowledge. I think he's selling them to make money. Either that, or he's being paid to stalk these women."

"Let's make sure we're right about that last part before anything drastic." Erin grabbed the laptop, firing it up.

"We don't find anything through a normal search." I pulled out my phone and called one of my buddies who conducts internet research for the Navy.

He answered on the first ring.

"I owe you a million times for this, but I'm going to send over a few images. Can you find out if they're being sold?"

"Give me five minutes," and he hung up.

I sent over about three, hoping that would be enough.

Never in a million years did I think I would find that when I searched his car. We were in the business of protecting people, and here he was, attacking them at their most vulnerable.

"Oh my god, Damon. I'm sorry." She squeezed my arm.

"Why are you sorry?"

"I know you didn't do it. But he was your friend. I know this hurts you to see as well." Her eyes softened.

Your kindness is astounding sometimes.

"Thank you. I wanted to tell you… well, I wanted to tell you regardless. But I wanted to get your advice. Normally, I would run straight to the police, and I feel compelled to do that. But… he's fighting for custody of his daughter. How do I ruin his chances at that?" I put my face in my hands.

"Damon…" she started, and I knew what she was going to say simply by the tone of her voice.

"I know."

"It's ultimately your choice. However, I want you to know that you're not taking away his chances at getting custody. Everything that happens is a byproduct of his choices. He's broken the law, and he's done bad things."

She's right. She's saying what I couldn't say out loud.

The phone rang.

"What did you find?"

"I found the exact pictures on a popular pay-for-images sex site. I'm sending it to you."

"Thanks, man. I appreciate this."

"Don't worry about it, anytime," and the phone went dead.

"I have to turn him in," I sighed, rubbing my eyes.

"Hey… come here." She pulled me in, the scent of her coconut and mint shampoo filling my nostrils.

I can't resist her anymore.

"Erin," I spoke her name softly, claiming her lips the minute she lifted her head.

Her hands moved to my arms, and my hand found her

ass. I cupped it tightly, laying her down on the couch behind us.

Our tongues intertwined as I began to slowly unbutton her shirt.

"Are you sure?" I checked with her.

"Yes, please don't stop, Damon," she breathed, her eyes sultry and dark.

The shirt fell to the sides of her arms, exposing her succulent and full breasts. My mouth found her nipple, sucking and tugging as she moaned in ecstasy. My cock throbbed as she gasped and twitched.

Fuck, this is heaven.

As I kept moving south, her hands yanked my hair, keeping me steady. I wanted to feel all of her body, but I took my time.

Planting kisses down her stomach, I stopped when I reached her pussy before devouring her with my tongue, using two fingers to apply pressure to her swollen clit.

So ready for me.

"Damon, don't stop. God, don't stop," she begged, as I felt the climax build in her body.

Enough. I have to have her.

I quickly undressed myself, leaving only my hard member positioned at her entrance. As I slid a condom on, I checked her eyes.

"Are you ready?"

"Yes, please," and she grabbed my hips, thrusting me forward as I entered her in one swift motion.

Erin matched my rhythm as I pounded in and out of her. Then I flipped her over onto her stomach and reentered her from behind.

She felt exquisite, like she was made for me. Our bodies fit together like two puzzle pieces.

"Ahh..." she cried.

"Shhh, stay still, baby." I wrapped my hands in her hair as I tugged it back.

I'm going to come soon.

"Damon, I'm close." Erin's voice was almost a whisper.

Me too, baby. Me too.

She cried out as I spilled into the condom, our bodies desperately trying to find our breath. Pulling out of her, I curled Erin into me as I kissed the back of her head.

"That was… something. Wow," she giggled, reaching her hand around her back to rub my arm.

"You're amazing."

"Damon…"

"Yeah?"

"I think I love you."

"You know, I think it's incredibly cliche to say that after sex," I joked, turning to her. "But I'm pretty sure I'm in love with you too. In fact, I'm sure of it. You are the calm to relax me after a hard day. We fit."

My smile reached from ear to ear.

"Man, this is unexpected." Erin stood, buttoning her shirt.

Tell me about it. She came in like a hurricane.

"Do you think you could come to the station with me? I need to get this off my conscience tonight," I asked.

"Absolutely."

Chapter Fifteen

ERIN

The police arrested Johnny that night. Damon was remanded to the station to record his official statement and hand over the pictures he took for evidence. He had texted me that he was sitting in one of the offices when Johnny was brought in.

Thankfully, he didn't see him. Apparently, he looked absolutely distraught, which was to be expected.

Even though he felt it was ultimately the right decision, he was devastated that he had to be the one who turned his friend in. The police told Johnny they had received an anonymous tip, but I think he would piece it together eventually, given that Damon had visited him that same morning.

The afternoon that he and I shared was nothing short of extraordinary. Never in my life had anyone made me feel that level of pleasure and passion before. Damon was refined, experienced, and above all, I loved him. I think I had known it before the mind-blowing sex, but the dual confession after was heartwarming.

I returned home after accompanying him to the station and hadn't seen him since, even when it became the following morning.

"Hello? Is everything okay?" I answered the phone.

"Of course, it is. I was just calling to see how you were doing. I miss you. Also, I heard through the grapevine about a rumor. I guess I wanted to see if it was true. Come by for lunch?" Cara inquired.

"I would love to. Can I bring anything?" My stomach turned in knots.

What rumor would she hear?

"Just your lovely self. See you in a few hours." Cara hung up.

"Erin, come down here!" my dad yelled.

Why doesn't anyone speak at a normal volume in this house?

"Coming." I skipped two stairs at a time as I made my way down.

The news was on as usual, and my parents were glued to television. On the screen was a picture of Damon's friend, Johnny. As I listened, the news reporter stated that he had been arrested for suspicion of stalking, unlawful surveillance, and distribution of pornography. However, they said that while vehemently denying the claims, he admitted to another crime: a break-in at a local coffee shop.

It was him.

A couple of puzzle pieces began to slide into place as it clicked for me. It made complete sense why the break-in didn't precisely fit into the murder scheme. It wasn't the same culprit. I wondered if Damon was out of the station yet.

"Sweetheart, do you see this? Isn't this the guy that

Damon was friends with? Look at all these charges against him." My dad shook his head.

It's bad, I know.

"I don't know how I didn't see it," Ellison spat.

He was angry.

"You didn't really know him. Why would you? He was new to town," I pointed out.

"I had met him once or twice when out with Damon. He seemed like a stand-up guy. Guess I was wrong," my brother said.

"That is a little alarming if this is who Damon associates himself with. I don't think you two should be hanging out anymore," my dad practically whispered.

What? That makes no sense.

"Dad… you can't be serious. Suddenly he's responsible for the actions of the people he knows? Do you hold everyone else to that ridiculously high standard?"

"Hey! You don't talk to me like that, young lady. I'm just looking out for you. This is our home, and even though you are an adult, we have certain rules. As of right now, I don't see a good reason why you should hang out with him."

My dad has never spoken to me like this either. The murders were toying with everyone's head.

"Dad, they're together. You can't expect them just to break up," Ellison protested, much to my dad's dismay and my surprise.

"Son, I don't care. That's my rule. Follow it, or you can leave." My dad stood and stormed off.

Only then did I notice the glass of whiskey sitting there. My dad hardly ever drank liquor, and when he did, it was clear he was struggling with something. My mom had stepped out momentarily to get some groceries earlier, so he probably overindulged.

"I don't even know what to say…" I sat there in disbelief.

"Erin, he's bluffing. And clearly, he's been drinking. Don't let what he says dictate you following your heart. That's equally as important. It'll blow over, I promise." Ellison kissed my head as he made his way to his room.

The gesture was probably the softest and purest form of love he had ever expressed towards me, and I know it was him feeling bad about my father giving me a hard time. My dad had always been strict as my being his only girl growing up, but he had never yelled at me or been so aggressive about his opinion before… especially when I was an adult.

Part of the reason he did so often was my father drilling in him since we were children the idea that "you have to be a man, and men don't cry." My father rarely cried, and I could count on one hand the number of times he cried in my entire life.

"Thanks, big brother. I'll see you later. I'm going to Cara's for lunch."

"Text when you get there," he yelled before I heard the door close.

As I started my Jeep, Damon pulled in.

Beep. Beep.

He turned at my horn and jogged over to the car. His usually neat hair was disheveled, and his eyes were bloodshot.

"Where are you off to?"

"Your sister invited me for lunch. She wants to clear the air about a rumor."

His eyebrow raised with curiosity.

"I wonder what that is. I was going to catch you up on everything that happened at the station, but we can do that later. Go enjoy yourself." Damon kissed me.

But I want to know what happened.

"Are you sure? I can reschedule. I have a lot I wanted to fill you in on, too."

"I'm sure, Erin. I know she misses her friend. Go get some girl time and pop by later. Besides, I'm wiped. I'll get some rest while you're gone."

"That sounds good. Hey, did you hear about the break-in news?"

A puzzled look crossed his exhausted face. "No. Did they find who it was?"

"Johnny. No reason as to why yet, but it was on the news."

"Shit. No, that's news to me. It makes a lot of sense, though. Alright, you get going. I'll see you later," he gave me another kiss and then was off.

I watched him get inside the house before I pulled away.

My lunch with Cara was a bit inconsequential until the end. We laughed about work horror stories, and mine didn't compare to hers. A desk job couldn't hold a candle to managing a classroom of twenty-five rambunctious kindergarteners.

"You have to tell me about the rumor you heard. I've been chomping at the bit. Spill." I took a sip of the Pinot Grigio she poured me. Jonas was doing overtime, and the kids were out with their grandparents for the day.

"Okay, fine. Someone mentioned that they had seen you and Damon out on the town. They saw you guys kiss. So tell me the truth… are you an item?"

This was it. It was the moment I was dreading. I had disappointed my brother and my father and was about to let down my best friend.

"Yes. Look, Cara—"

She waved her hand, cutting me off.

"Erin, you're my best friend in the entire world. You always have been. Damon's my brother. If you thought I would ever have any reaction other than complete support for the two of you finding happiness, I'm sorry I have given you that impression."

My heart is soaring.

"I'm so glad to hear that. I have been nervous for days over how you would react."

"Please! My kids need some cousins to play with. It's about time someone snatched him up. The fact that it is someone as awesome as you is comforting."

I pulled her into a hug as I wiped the tears from my eyes.

Chapter Sixteen

DAMON

My heart is thundering in my chest. Shouts erupt from all sides of me. The debris is too thick on my face. I can't see.
Help!
I can't see. I can't breathe.
"Damon!" Erin shook me awake.

Sweat was pouring down my body, my hair a matted mess on my head. I hadn't experienced a nightmare as vivid as that one in some time. Having Erin next to me helped. She relaxed me. Erin had been spending the night here and there, but it was slowly becoming more of a regular arrangement. Her dad was pretty much staying out of it at this point. He was neither angry nor was he doing backflips at our budding relationship.

"Was it a nightmare?" she prompted, her eyes creased with worry.

"Yeah." I took a deep breath, glancing at the clock.

It was nearly five in the morning, and light was beginning to trickle into the sky.

"Is it the same one every time?"

"No. They're all different. Usually, they're some kind of flashback to my time with the SEALs but with changes. This one... this one was dark. I still feel like I can feel the debris on me." I wiped my face.

Better go get the run in now... clear my mind.

"I'm going to go for a run. I can't sleep now anyways." I stood, slipping my dog tags around my neck.

They went everywhere with me. Even when I wore a suit or a nice outfit, there they were. They were pieces of me, and it felt wrong to go out without them. They would hang on the bedside table lamp during my sleep, and when I woke, they went right back on.

"I'll come." She pulled the covers off herself.

"No, you stay. Get some rest. It's our day off, enjoy. I'll be back soon." I kissed her, leaving the warmth of the shared bed to the harsh cold of the early morning.

Music played in my ears as my feet thudded on the cold, hard cement underneath me. It was deathly quiet. The only light was the early emerging sun coupled with the street lights. My growing frustration with the investigation was being taken out through my punishing pace.

As I rounded the corner of one of the industrial areas, a shot went off. Instantly, I dropped to the ground and began to look around. I couldn't immediately see anything, but another round went off, and I could hear it from the right of me. Suddenly, someone in a hoodie ran out of the building and sprinted down the street. Their neon green shoes flashed under the scattered streetlights.

I wanted to chase after them, to apprehend them. My instinct told me otherwise. I needed to see what happened... if there were more bodies in the building.

More murders.

Once the man was out of sight, my feet hit the ground running. The building had cobwebs plastering the entrance. Turning on the flashlight on my phone, I slowly walked through the floors, clearing every room. It appeared to be abandoned. Each room had some equipment left behind that clearly hadn't been used in years.

When I approached the third floor, I saw a puddle slowly forming from under the second door to my right, a stream entering the hallway.

Bingo.

Inside, a body lay in a slump on the floor. They were on their stomach, hands splayed at their sides. Blood pooled around them, stemming from two wounds on their back.

He was killed.

I didn't want to disturb the body, but I needed to see who it was. My flashlight flickered over their face.

I recognized him as Aaron Cole. He was a deputy I went to high school with and a decent cop. None of this made any sense. All of the victims were women, up until this point, killed by strangulation. This was far from that.

My heart was beating fast, adrenaline coursing through me. I released my fist that I didn't realize I was clenching and dialed the police.

Within minutes, they had arrived and secured the crime scene. They took a lengthy and detailed statement before letting me go. Erin's phone calls began to ring in slowly as I was being questioned, and I had to silence them. I hadn't thought about it in the moment, but she was probably sick with worry.

"Hi, I'm sorry I didn't answer," I doled out apologies as she answered the phone on the first ring.

"It's okay. I was just worried. You've been gone for a long time now. Are you okay?"

"It's a long story. I'm almost home now. I'm getting a ride back to the house. I'll explain when I see you."

"A ride? Okay, I'm waiting. I've got coffee on."

Deputy Briars dropped me off in front of the house as he waved me off.

He hadn't said a word the entire drive, no doubt grief-stricken by seeing a fellow officer dead. I gave my condolences once more as I closed the door behind me. Erin was standing at the front door with two cups of coffee. Once she noticed the police car, her face went pale.

Don't worry, sweetheart. I'm okay.

"I have a million and one questions," she started, handing me the coffee.

"I have answers. Let's go inside, come on."

I ran her through the details of my early morning run as she listened in horror. Her face was sick with worry, and her hand squeezed mine tightly. She wasn't as hardened to these kinds of things as I was. I could see the fear in her eyes, and everything in me wanted to take it away. I knew I could keep her safe. I just needed her near me.

"What does this all mean, Damon? I mean… you and I both know that after all these kills, straying from the victim profile like that is off. Something's going on."

I nodded in agreement. I had already considered it as I ran through it in my head once more on the drive home.

"You're right. You tell me. What do you think this behavior is exhibiting?"

"Honestly… a crime of opportunity. A male deputy is nowhere near their usual victim profile. They likely killed him because they had to."

"I agree. But why? Did he discover who they were?" I tapped my chin.

"He probably did."

She shook her head in frustration, laying it on me. It felt good and comforting.

It's only been two weeks of her being here at my home. But I know what I want.

"I have a question for you. I know it's fast, and we just started dating. But I'm not a kid. I know what I want in life, and since you came to town, I want you. I want you to be safe, and I know I can do that if you're here with me. Move in, please?" My eyes were pleading, and hers softened.

She jumped onto my lap, hugging me tightly, despite the fact that I smelled like garbage and my sweat was now cold and left me with a soaked shirt.

"Yes. Of course. But does that mean I don't get to watch you undress from across the window anymore?" She feigned a frown, then giggled.

Oh, she's cheeky today.

"Unfortunately not, but I can peer at you from behind the shower curtains if that helps." I burst into laughter, and Erin slapped my arm playfully.

"Okay… today's darkness aside, how will we lighten the mood? It is our day off, after all."

"Maybe you could look around the house and start giving your input on decor? I know it looks like a bachelor pad, but I want you to feel comfortable here," I smiled.

It was about time for Erin to get a grown-up place. She wasn't jumping at the idea when she moved back to town, given the murders. But now that we were together, it just made sense.

"Really? You wouldn't mind me changing up your house?"

"It's ours. You live here now, remember?" I touched her chin, and we kissed.

A knock at the door interrupted us before we could go any further.

"Nobody's home!" I shouted as I made my way to the door, which only made the knocking louder.

"I'm coming, I'm coming." I yanked it open.

"Ellison." I eyed Erin's brother, who stood there looking panicked.

"Is Erin here?"

"She is. What's going on?"

"I just wanted to know she was safe. There was another murder." He wiped a bead of sweat off of his forehead.

"Yeah, I know. Come in, man. I'll fill you in." I opened the door wide as he stepped in, his eyes scanning the room.

"Ellison? What are you doing here?" Erin emerged from around the corner.

"I wanted to check on you and make sure you were okay. The news said there was another murder. A deputy this time?"

"Yeah, man. It was Aaron Cole."

Ellison's face fell. They were close in high school. I wasn't sure how much they were in contact now, but the news clearly devastated him. He sat on the couch and put his face in his hands, shaking his head from side to side.

"I know. Look, we'll get this son of a bitch. I promise," I said, taking a seat next to him. I put my arm around him comfortingly.

"My mom is freaked out. My dad is on a tear, too. He's not really coping well with all this going on." He shot a look towards Erin.

I knew what her dad had said. He didn't want her around me because of what Johnny had done. I had known the man most of my life, but fear did something strange to people. Most of the time, it warped their personalities into fight or flight mode. He was doing everything in his power to protect his family... but it still stung.

"Everyone is. Here, come take a look at this." I pulled Ellison up and led him to my office, where I had the board with all the investigation findings pinned up.

His eyes grew wide, and then a sly smile formed at the corner of his lip.

"I knew you weren't doing nothing. This is great, Damon. I want to help in any way that I can."

I wouldn't mind that. Any help was better than none. Maybe then their dad would come to his senses and see that I had nothing to do with what was going on.

"Who's Andrew?" He pointed to the paper I had pinned up with the background check into

Him.

"He's someone new in town. Your sister had a run-in with him a few times and got a bad vibe. All I could find was a restraining order from his ex-girlfriend. It was probably a messy breakup, and he went a little crazy."

He tapped his chin deep in thought as Erin came in, holding two cups of coffee for us. Ellison wrapped his arm around her sideways as he kissed her forehead. The gesture was odd for them, given their usual tumultuous relationship. However, with everything they had been going through lately as a family, I knew it meant a lot to Erin.

Her eyes met mine, and I winked as I lifted the coffee cup to my lips.

Thanks, baby.

"I just had an idea. Did you reach out to the ex-girlfriend at all?" Ellison set his cup down and pulled the paper off of the board.

"No, I didn't. Why? What are you thinking?"

"These background checks don't include everything. You should reach out to her for the full story on why the restraining order was placed. Then, we can see if this Andrew fellow is a real threat."

"You're right. I'll try and find a phone number for her right now," I said as I sat down at my desk, opening my laptop.

Ellison pulled Erin into the hallway for a hushed conversation that I couldn't quite make out, but judging from her look, it was nothing but positive.

When they reentered, I had just found the phone number for Andrews's ex-girlfriend Poppy. She wasn't too far.

I picked up the phone.

Chapter Seventeen

ERIN

Having Ellison's support was everything. It hurt that I didn't have my dad's, but my mom assured me that she was working on him. Everything within me knew deep down that his reaction was fear-based, driven merely by love and the need to protect those around him. I also knew from my education that I was still okay and even allowed to feel angry with him for his reaction—which I was.

I stepped away while Damon called Andrew's ex-girlfriend to set up a meeting or even get more information over the phone. I didn't want to intrude on the two of them having boy time.

Damon had been spending every free moment with me lately, and I knew my brother was likely missing his buddy. Being the same age, they had always been close friends. Besides, it gave me more time to work on my profile.

My latest speculation was that the killer was in a position of authority... possibly a judge, a teacher, or even someone higher up at work. We didn't exactly have a long list of power positions in this small town. I had determined this primarily due to the victim type and the brutality of the kills. It struck me as the kind of person who had to keep themselves composed and professional most of the day and who snapped and went "dark" in their kills.

I started compiling a list of people I knew were in a position of power. Cara was obviously off the list of teachers, and I was primarily looking at males, anyway.

The school website was gracious enough to have a current list of all their educators listed, so I made a list of the male teachers.

Moving on from school, I checked the judges in their area using our online judicial informant system. There were only two.

I then realized that, quite possibly, the biggest group of people in power was our police station. It couldn't have been a coincidence that one of them was found murdered this morning.

My mind started to drift, focusing heavily on the "why" of the events that transpired today.

Why was he killed?

Did he know something he shouldn't? Find out something?

Did he become a liability?

Or was it a familiar case of the wrong place at the wrong time?

Ellison and Damon emerged from the office looking grim.

Oh, God. What is it?

"Well?" I prompted.

"She was more than happy to volunteer information to us, and she was willing to meet if we wanted." Damon poured himself some coffee.

"The reason she filed the restraining order was exactly as it stated, due to threats and stalking, but it left something out." Ellison grabbed a cup alongside Damon.

"And? What was it? You're leaving me in suspense here," I shot, annoyed at their coyness.

"He would show up to her job. Threatened coworkers, called her boss; it was crazy." Damon took a sip, eyes leveled at the floor.

Fuck. That's not good.

"I guess we have our killer," Ellison chimed in.

I wouldn't be too sure of that.

"Let's not seal his fate yet, no matter how scummy he is. Look at this here." I passed them the list.

"You think it's someone in a position of power?" Ellison laughed, not sold on the idea.

"Yes… starting with the police department."

My brother's eyes turned to slits as he advanced toward me. He grabbed my arms, his grip tight and angry.

"You're not going to sit here and make up lies about one of the respected members of this town. He was a hero!"

I wasn't looking at his friend like a suspect.

"I didn't mean him! But maybe his brothers in blue aren't as esteemed as they claim to be. Maybe he found out something that he shouldn't have. I know this is hard for you to grasp, but sometimes people aren't how they seem, Ellison!"

He hadn't let me go yet, and Damon took notice. As he set his glass down, my brother stepped back, hands in the air.

"You're right. I'm sorry. His death is hitting me hard. It just doesn't seem fair, why good people have to keep dying. I'm sick of everyone dying." He wiped a stray tear from his eye, turning to the side so we couldn't see.

You don't always have to bottle up your emotions.

I pulled him in for a hug, and he reciprocated immediately, his hands wrapping around my back, pulling tight.

"I love you. I'm always here for you," I proclaimed.

"I know. I know," he repeated.

"Not to intrude on the family moment here, but I'm here for both of you- in case it needs to be said," Damon joked, to which he earned a playful slap from me.

His smoldering eyes met mine, and I felt myself on fire. As selfish as it felt, I yearned for my brother to excuse himself and head back home.

"Alright, I just came over to check and make sure you were okay. I'll leave you to it. Mom and Dad are probably worried about me. And Erin, reach out to dad. You know he's far more stubborn than he'd ever admit... but he misses you."

I knew it.

"I will... bye." I released him from the hug, and he shook Damon's hand then headed for the door.

Did he really need to get home, or did he sense the tension between us?

Damon turned to me the second the door closed and grabbed me, placing me on the kitchen counter behind us. His hands wandered my body as he landed soft, tender kisses on my shoulder blades.

Shit, that feels good. I want him, now.

My hands gently pulled his hair back as I returned the favor, focusing on his neck. A moan escaped his lips.

Damon yanked up on my shirt, pulling it over my head. Using his right hand, he pushed me onto my back as he carefully shimmied my pants down.

"No panties... just for me." He splayed his hands on my thighs, spreading them wide as he dove in, his tongue teasing me as I exploded in ecstasy.

"God, Damon. Your mouth is amazing," I moaned, gripping the counter edge.

Damon started planting soft kisses on my thighs as his fingers eased inside of me. My back arched in response, and his other hand found my clit, rubbing it in a circular motion.

"Do you like the way I feel inside you?" His fingers curled, and I moaned in response.

He stood, removing his shorts in one quick motion. He checked my face for confirmation before entering me in one thrust.

Fuck.

"You feel so good," I said as he flexed forward, pumping in and out.

My fingernails dug into his back as his hips circled, leaving my toes curled in ecstasy.

Our mouths found each other, his teeth settling on my lip as he gave it a gentle tug.

I'm so close. He feels amazing.

"Erin, I'm about to…" he groaned, his hair plastered on his forehead with a bead of sweat.

He flipped me over, and I was on top as he folded his arms behind his head.

"I thought you were about to finish," I breathed, riding him up and down as his fingers dug into my ass, guiding me.

"You feel too good. I wanted more." His hands roamed my breasts, gently tugging my nipples.

I never want this to end.

"Damon!" I screamed as I felt his cock throb inside me, his moans echoing through the room.

"You're amazing. Has anyone ever told you that?" I joked, catching my breath.

"Oh, yeah. Plenty of girls," he chuckled, pulling his

shorts back up.

Before I could retort, he spun me once and dipped me, planting a kiss on my lips.

"None of them were as stunning and interesting as you, however. None compared."

Can you say swoon?

"You make me feel like I'm on a cloud... weightless and—"

"High?"

"Mr. Funny today, huh? You know what I mean. I'm starving. Let's go get some breakfast?"

"Are you sure? With the murder this morning?" He eyed me carefully.

"I feel safe with you. Let's go to Caribous," I smiled, grabbing the car keys.

"You got it, baby."

I quickly dressed and met him in the car, and we drove to the local mom-and-pop diner. Nothing would make me feel better than some good old-fashioned comfort food. Caribou's was run by Al and Mary, and it had been in their family for generations. Last I heard, their two kids were also working there, gearing up to run the shop when their parents were ready to retire.

"For two?" A bright-eyed waitress greeted us as we strolled in. She was adorned in the classic white frilled apron and bright red t-shirt. Her name tag read *Fern*.

"Yes, ma'am," Damon returned, and she blushed instantly.

You get ogles everywhere we go.

Sitting down in the familiar booths brought me back to my time as a child, coming here with my family. Back then, it was a treat to go and eat out with the family as we didn't have much money growing up. We always got shakes and an appetizer combo to share between the four of us. It held such fond memories, even now.

"Hi folks, what'll it be today?" The server approached us, pen and notepad at the ready.

"I think I'll go with the bacon and eggs breakfast plate, hash browns, and fruit, please." Damon closed his menu and handed it to the waitress.

"I'll have the chicken fried steak with fruit and wheat toast; thanks." I did the same.

My mouth was practically salivating at my order, and it hadn't even been put into the system yet. She quickly retreated and returned with the complimentary cups of coffee and water.

As we sat and giggled about the morning tryst, Andrew walked in, his typical attire gone. Instead of the jacket that shielded his face, he wore a plain white t-shirt, sweats, and these very loud, bright green shoes.

"Damon… look." I nodded in his direction.

The hostess led Andrew to a booth directly in view of ours. As Damon turned to see who I was referring to, his face paled. He immediately picked up his phone and started typing. My phone chimed in front of me, and I glanced at the screen.

Damon: Erin, it's him. He killed the deputy.

Erin: What? How do you know?

Damon: His shoes. I remember seeing them when the killer ran away from the scene. They were the same bright shoes.

Erin: What do we do?

Damon: I text the sheriff. And we sit here and enjoy our food like nothing is wrong.

We both put our phones down as they brought out our steaming plates of food. My belly grumbled, and Damon rubbed his hands together excitedly. Out of the corner of my eye, I caught Andrew taking notice of us. He stared, but I wouldn't give the satisfaction of looking his way. If Damon was right, he was a killer.

Knowing that nugget of information only sparked my curiosity further. Why in the world would he kill the deputy? Did the deputy find out something about him? I felt like that was the safest bet. There's no way that Andrew could have been the killer of the female victims, though. He didn't fit the profile we had been working on, as incomplete as it was. Damon felt strongly that it was someone in a position of power. Of course, I had no actual idea what job he had. I don't know. Maybe it was a gut feeling. But Damon felt sure about the shoes and his profile. I had to trust in his judgment.

The first bite was as delicious as I thought it would be. But my appetite waned suddenly when I looked out the window. Officers pulled into the parking lot, at least five cars that I could see. No other diner, including Damon, had taken notice of their presence. But I was watching them intently.

One by one, officers slowly exited the car, in no rush at all. Their faces, however, told a different story. Each of them looked grim, clearly on a mission.

They were here for Andrew.

They filed in slowly, hands on their hips as we continued to eat. The waitress had shuffled over to Andrew's table and was taking his order as they had him stand and place his hands behind his back.

His eyes locked with mine as they read him his rights, and he looked genuinely fearful.

Is Damon wrong? No, he can't be.

Maybe it was remorse.

And then he was gone.

"Don't feel bad, Erin. He's a killer, and now he's put away." Damon popped a piece of egg into his mouth. He started furiously typing on his phone, and I caught Ellison's name on the screen.

He would be relieved to know that his friend's killer had been arrested. I was also happy, but equal parts stressed because the real killer, the real *threat*, had not been found yet.

Chapter Eighteen

DAMON

It was all over the news. The headlines read, *Police Killer Caught*, more information to follow. There were no significant details released as of yet. The general public wasn't even aware of the identity. But I was, as were Ellison and Erin.

I was wracked with the why, and so was Ellison. The death had completely wrecked him, and now that he knew who had done it, he was even more curious as to why. I was too, however.

Erin was convinced that the officer found something out about Andrew, and that's why he killed him. Perhaps the officer did a little digging on his own with the resources he had and found out the reason for Andrew's restraining order placement. He might have threatened to take his findings public, anointing him as the first suspect. Andrew was done for in the public eye if that happened. Our town was so scared, and they needed someone to be responsible. They would believe anything at this point.

Was that reason enough to kill someone? Was that reason enough to take the life of a distinguished officer—to fit in?

I had barely been able to sleep all night, my nightmares keeping me up and tossing and turning. I accumulated a total of around three hours of sleep. It was the weekend, and I only had one day left before it was time to return to work. Despite everything going on, my only true plan was to lay in bed and make love to Erin all day.

On the other hand, she was determined to figure out the cause behind Andrew's killing of the officer. Some part of her felt that it connected to the other murders, but I wasn't convinced. She had spent the better part of the previous evening piecing together and finalizing her profile on the killer. She was convinced more than ever that it was an officer. They always seemed to be one step ahead; they were physically strong, and they knew how not to leave a trace of DNA behind.

Say that it was true. If it was, did Andrew come to the same conclusion and suspect it was our friend? Was it really him? Was he protecting another brother in blue who was the real killer? Of course, this was all just the result of my mind working overtime, and nothing could be proven. All the answers seemed unlikely, but I decided to humor Erin anyway. She tended to be right about most things, as it was.

Slipping my dog tags on, I decided to go for a run to clear my head before what was sure to be another exhausting investigative day.

"Please don't witness any more murders, please," Erin called from the bathroom as she brushed her teeth.

"I'll do my best! Be back soon." I shut the door behind

me and started sprinting, music flooding my ears and letting me shut my brain off.

My feet hit the pavement underneath me when the music cut abruptly and a phone call came in. It was a number I didn't recognize. Typically, those kinds of calls are directly ignored. But something inside me pushed me to answer it.

"Hello?" I came to a screeching halt.

"No time, no see, old friend," Johnny's voice poured from the other end.

Oh, boy.

"Johnny. How are you, man? I heard about everything," I feigned sympathy, but I knew he was smarter than that.

"Oh, cut the shit, Damon. You turned me in. You know it and I know it. There's no reason to suggest otherwise, right?"

"You're right. I won't lie to you. You were doing some fucked up shit. You were a drunk, and you were breaking the law. You were invading people's privacy. The naked photos? C'mon, Johnny, it's not you," I spat. Everything in me that I had suppressed saying to him came bubbling out.

"I know. Trust me, I know. You did the right thing. It still hurts, because we were friends. You're definitely a better man than I am, that's for sure."

Where's this going?

"I appreciate that. So, what's the call for?"

"I need a favor, and in return, I have something that I think you would like to hear."

He's bullshitting.

"What's the information?"

"First, I need your promise that you'll keep your word on the favor," he pleaded, and I knew right then that he was serious.

"You have my word, Johnny."

"Keep an eye on my daughter, would you? They're moving me to the actual county prison tomorrow, and I know I won't be getting out anytime soon. Check in on her every once in a while. Make sure she's living a good life."

That's the Johnny that I remember.

"You got it."

"Now, as for what I wanted to call you about. I'm still in the police station right now, getting moved tomorrow. My new cellmate had a lot to vent about today…"

"Andrew?" My eyes grew wide.

"Word around here is that he killed a cop. Station is pissed. But he says it was self-defense."

No way.

"That doesn't make any sense. Why would he need to defend himself?" I questioned.

"Who knows how true this is, but Andrew says that the cop tried to kill him first. He said that the cop threatened him to stay away from Erin, that she wasn't his to play with," Johnny whispered.

My blood ran cold.

"What, he was hers?"

"No, he wanted to keep Andrew away from Erin. But not for him, for his boss. Look, I have to go. But you had to know. Do with it what you will, and hey, please keep true to your promise, man."

The line went dead, and I took a seat on the curb to try to steady myself. This was all about Erin. Andrew's run-ins with my girlfriend had made someone angry enough to try and mill him for it. Our cop friend wasn't the mastermind; he was only an errand boy. So, who was the real killer?

And why hadn't I been targeted? Andrew had flirted with Erin a few times, sure. But he wasn't dating her. He wasn't sleeping with her. It didn't make any sense.

Suddenly, I didn't need the run anymore. I had enough adrenaline to last me the rest of the day. My walk home was slow-paced, purposefully calculated to give me enough time to sort through possibilities and next steps in my head.

If it was all true, it was possible the "boss" was someone who worked at the station. The captain, perhaps? I shuddered at the thought. He's been in the position for so long that it seemed irritational, if not irresponsible, for me to view him in that way, given that I had zero evidence.

"Hey, you!" Erin shouted from the patio as I strolled up.

I was beginning to think that my runs were simply bad luck. A break in the case was usually a good thing, but news like this wasn't great to hear about my girlfriend. I was more worried than ever for her safety. If someone was willing to kill people who had come in contact with her, then not only was she in danger from a lunatic, but so was everyone she associated with.

I didn't worry for myself. I could handle myself just fine. Instead, I found myself anxious over the safety of my sister and her family, Ellison, his mom and dad, and even Charles, who had taken a liking to Erin lately.

In fact, Charles had been a little over-friendly with her at work. It was nothing too alarming or anything that raised major red flags, but at this point, everything was worth a second look.

"Hi…" I paused.

"What is it? Don't tell me you saw another body…" She covered her mouth.

"No, it's actually a little worse. Let's go inside. I need a shower."

She switched the shower on and joined me in undressing as we both popped in the shower. Erin soaped up the loofah and began to rub it over my body as she eyed me, looking worried.

"Out with it," she probed.

"I got a call from Johnny. His cellmate is Andrew, who had a lot to say about what happened. According to him, he was threatened to stop talking to you and had an attempted kill on him. In self-defense, he killed the officer and fled."

Erin's skin went pale, and her eyes shifted nervously. She hadn't expected it to be concerning her.

"Wait, what? It's about me? I barely knew the officer."

"He was merely a pawn, working for a bigger fish. Now his boss… he's the one who's got his eyes set on you," I practically whispered, not even wanting to say the words aloud.

The thought of anyone hurting Erin pained me deeply. She had become increasingly important to me in such a short time. I was fully willing to fight tooth and nail to ensure her safety.

"His boss? Who the hell is that? I just got back in town… who would have it out for me?" She sighed, running her hand through her hair.

"Erin… breathe. I know it's a lot to take in. But believe me when I say this, I won't let *anything* happen to you. Nobody is touching you."

"So, what do we do with this? Do we tell the police department?"

Naturally, yes. But circumstances now have me questioning otherwise.

"Honestly, if what Johnny said checks out, then there's corruption in the police department. I can't be sure who's in on it and who isn't. If we tell them we know, there could be some serious consequences. I vote for keeping it to ourselves for now. Erin?" I eyed her, pushing for her decision.

It was ultimately hers.

"Yeah. That sounds like the smart thing to do. I trust you, Damon."

"I trust you too. Implicitly."

"I know we're basically under the watchful eye of a serial killer, my friend just got arrested, your brother's friend was a crooked cop, and there's corruption in our local law enforcement, but what do you say we take the night off from sleuthing? Get some rest in?"

Work was back tomorrow, and God knew I needed the relaxation.

"That sounds… heavenly," she purred, rubbing shampoo into my hair.

Her eyes were seductive and reflective, but behind that was hidden fear and anxiety. Everything in me wanted to take it away from her, to make it all better. But here I was, feeling useless for the first time. Right now, the best thing I could do for her was stand by her side and be there for her. It was a tough pill for me to swallow. I was never the sit-and-do-nothing guy. I charged forward, took control, and fought against what was wrong.

As we sat on the couch with a fresh bowl of popcorn and two sodas, reruns of Gilmore Girls turned on. Erin squealed in delight.

God, not the Gilmore girls. Anything but.

Her face panned to mine, and she instantly turned the channel.

"Sorry, we can watch something else."

Hell no. I don't ever want to be responsible for that look.

"Nope. Let's watch it," and I settled back into the couch.

A few hours later, I peeled open my eyes to find we had

both dozed off on the couch. The TV was blaring, so I switched it off and began to turn off all the lights.

As I peered out of the front window, I could make out a figure standing in the distance.

What the hell?

Unlocking the door, I pulled it open slowly, trying to focus on who it was.

"Hey, get out of here!"

They didn't move.

I reached for my gun in the safe to the right of the door. But when I looked back up, they were gone.

Chapter Nineteen

ERIN

"Wake up, we need to go," Damon said as he shook me awake.

Groggy as I was, I stood up and quickly dressed, grabbing my phone as we left in a hurry. Damon drove us to a nearby hotel, checking us in under a random name unrelated to his.

By the time we reached our room, I was fully awake and had a million and one questions.

"First, what the hell is going on, Damon?"

He sat on the bed beside me, taking my hand in his.

"There was someone at the house. I think they're coming after you, and this was the quickest way I could think of to get you somewhere safe." He gestured to our king-sized room.

"What do you mean? Who was it?"

"When I was locking up the house, I noticed someone standing down the driveway, just staring at the house. I went to grab my gun, and then they were gone. Taking a chance on staying there didn't sound like a good idea."

But my parents. Ellison.

"But if this person is really after me, don't you think they're going to try and hurt the people in my life? My brother isn't safe, and neither are my parents. We have to go back for them!"

"Erin, your brother is well-trained. He can keep them safe. I already texted him and gave him a brief idea of what was happening. You, however, seem to be the next target for this killer, and I'll be damned if I let anything happen to you." His eyes scanned mine, desperately looking for me to confirm his actions.

They were done out of love.

"Okay… you're right. And why can't we call the police?"

"I think they're corrupted, you know that. Not all of them, of course, but who's to say the person I talk to when I call won't be the killer himself?"

Also true.

I laid back on the bed, staring at the ceiling. I was wide awake now. My adrenaline rush had kicked in, and the fear was pushed to the side. I was furious as I dealt with the idea that a killer was coming after me.

Sure, I felt safe with Damon. That wasn't a question. He made me feel safe all the time. It was the idea that I couldn't just live my life. I felt like I had to look over my shoulder everywhere I went, and that was not something I ever wanted to feel.

"What's the game plan? We can't stay locked up here."

"Well, it's Monday. We have work in a few hours. I know it's probably the last thing on your mind right now, but I do have to go in, and I would feel a lot more comfortable knowing that you're safe in the building where I can protect you. Should we try and get a few more hours of sleep?"

As if I could sleep now.

"I don't want to stay here anyway. I want to work. But honestly, I don't even know if I could sleep right now. My heart feels like it's beating a million miles a minute."

"Same here. But we're safe, I promise. Do you want to relax and watch some television?"

"Sure."

As we lay together in the early morning hours, Damon did his best to put on a happy face for me. It was easy to see through it, though. He was nervous but didn't want that worry to fall onto me. Once the alarm clock went off, indicating it was time for work, Damon huddled in the bathroom, getting dressed. I took my sweet time, not wanting to deal with the catastrophic situation I found myself in.

The drive to work was quiet. I could sense Damon trying to piece together a real plan. He knew we couldn't stay at a hotel under a fake name forever. Allowing him to follow his process, I closed my eyes, listening to the hum of the radio.

"Good luck at work," he said as he kissed me, and we went our separate ways to our offices at work.

Work was a welcome distraction today. I had too much on my mind, and with this, I could push it to the back for as long as I could.

The day felt slightly monotonous, and I hadn't seen Damon since we arrived. Mondays were usually pretty busy for the office, especially with the weekend requests that came piling in. Knowing him, he was likely on e-mail duty and furiously replying to all the emails that he could.

A text rolled in around noon, and I found myself smiling. He liked to text me around lunchtime and see if I wanted to join him in his office.

But it wasn't from Damon.

It was an unknown number.

Shame I didn't get to see you this morning.

My fingers hit the keys, angrily typing a reply.

Erin: What the fuck do you want from me?

An instant reply came in.

Isn't it obvious, Erin? I want you. Do you think that leaving the house will protect you?

Erin: Damon will kill you.

Aw, he probably could. But then who would protect Ellison or your mother? Maybe even your father. Erin, I could hurt every single person in your life if you want to play that game. Or…

Erin: Or what?

Turn yourself over to me. Willingly.

Fuck. I set my phone down. He was right. Damon could defend himself… even me if he had to. But my mother, my father? I couldn't allow the people I loved to be victims because of some insane infatuation with me.

Erin: How do you want to do this?

Get in the red sedan parked outside your work. I'll see you soon.

My heart was beating. I could beat this. I could beat him, whoever it was. This was the only way to keep the people I loved safe. It fell on me to be the one to bring down this evil that had ruled our town for much too long.

I peered out of the office door. Damon was nowhere in sight, and Charles was absent from his desk.

It's go time.

I quickly slid the pepper spray and taser that Damon got me the other day into the back waistband of my jeans. I sure as hell was going to be prepared.

I wouldn't be another victim.

I slipped into the elevator, feeling my heart rage as it descended.

Cassandra waved me off with a smile as we licked gazes.

If only you knew.

Sure enough, the texts were right. There was a red sedan parked north of the entrance, the engine idling. I could make out someone sitting in the front driver's seat, but nobody else.

How do you know they won't have someone hiding in the back, ready to bombard you?

I guess I didn't. However, there weren't many choices.

As my hand opened the door, I saw a police officer sitting inside. He was immediately recognizable, but his name tag read Edwards. He had a grim look, as if he didn't want to be doing this either.

"So, it's you?" I asked, breaking the silence as I climbed in.

He's not hiding who he is. Maybe I'm as good as dead.

"No. You'll meet him soon." He hit the child lock button and started off, peeling out of the parking lot.

Maybe he'll get pulled over for his high speed. Then again, Edwards will flash his police badge and be on our way.

"Where are we going?"

"No more questions. Be quiet," he said as he turned onto a long dirt road.

An industrial-looking building came into view. Was it the same one that Damon witnessed a murder at the other night? It couldn't be.

Edwards yanked me out of the car, and I stumbled over my feet. My hair fell in my face as I hit the dirt.

"Come on, get up." He pulled me back onto my feet.

Securing my hands behind my back, he handcuffed me.

Please don't find the pepper spray or taser in my waistband.

Surprisingly enough, he didn't. It was the one time I felt grateful for an incompetent police officer.

Edwards didn't say anything as he led me into the building. We climbed two sets of stairs until we were at the very top of the building's third floor.

Is he going to push me to my death?

Instead, there was a chair in the center of the room. I was pushed onto it as he quickly secured my hands and feet to it using rope.

"You can go, Edwards. I've got it from here," a voice called from the shadows.

No. God, please, no.

Jonas emerged, a sinister look on his face. He looked a bit messy, but it didn't seem to affect his mood one bit. It all felt a little victorious, like he had won.

I've known him since I was younger. He was Cara's high school sweetheart. They had children together. How could he do this?

The drawings. Lila was trying to show me something.

"You seem surprised. I thought for sure that my daughter's drawing would tip you off. Instead, it made you and my wife argue. I wanted to kill her right then and there," he huffed, rage building.

"Jonas… this doesn't make any sense. You're not a killer. You can't be."

"Oh, anyone can be anything; you should know that. As a behavior analyst, I would assume that you would have pieced it together by now. After all, I texted you."

The behavior profile I made matches him to a T. I can't believe I haven't seen it yet.

He was recently promoted to a higher position where he was now in charge of many people. He was someone who had to hold it in throughout the day—at work, as a dad, as a husband—and he let it out on his victims.

"Why? Why do you kill? So many women… and the police officers! You've roped them into your schemes, too. An officer is dead because of you. That death is on your head, too!"

His face twisted into a scowl. He didn't like what I was saying, and I didn't care. It was all true. I couldn't believe he would do this to Cara and his kids. He was a wolf in sheep's clothing in the truest sense of the phrase.

"No. That death is on that freak, Andrew. He should've shot him right when he arrived."

"Is that what you're going to do to me? Kill me like all of your other victims?"

"No… you're special." He ran his hand on my cheek, to which I jerked away violently.

His hand connected with my cheek again, sending my head to the side.

"Behave."

"What's your plan here? You have a wife and kids to go home to. Damon will find you. This doesn't end well for you."

"It's not about me. It's about us. You're the one I want. These women, they meant nothing. Cara means nothing," he shrugged.

"They were *people*. Their lives meant something, and you took them away. I won't let you do the same to me."

"Oh, love. You don't have a choice," and he walked away.

Chapter Twenty

DAMON

Erin was gone. The day had gotten away from me, and I wasn't able to check in on her once. I even missed lunch.

When I rounded her office at the end of the work day, her desk was empty. Her stuff had been left behind, so I waited for ten minutes. Then I checked the internal system and saw she hadn't clicked out either.

Her phone was sitting on the desk. I momentarily struggled with the ethics issue of going through my girlfriend's phone but then tossed it out as a non-issue once I realized she might be in serious trouble.

The thought of her in trouble made me practically ill. It also made me particularly angry. Having her here with me at work was supposed to help keep her safe all day, yet she was missing. I gave myself a mental kick for not checking in on her.

This is all my fault. If she's in trouble, it's because I failed to protect her.

My mouth dropped wide open as I read the most recent text thread between Erin and an unknown number. She had given herself over to the killer. Knowing Erin, she weighed the options he was giving her and went with the one that would keep all her family and friends safe. It was likely an empty threat. A small part of me was angry that she went along with it. How could she purposefully put herself in danger when I was planning on keeping her safe?

I didn't fare well with things that felt out of my control, and this entire situation felt widely out of control.

"Charles, you didn't happen to see Erin today, did you?" I shouted at my assistant, who was packing up his briefcase.

"I saw her when she came in, but then I haven't seen her since. Normally, she pops out for some coffee midday, but she didn't today."

Fuck. This isn't good.

I dialed Cara, and she answered on the first ring.

"Hi, big brother, what's up?" She sounded especially chipper.

"Is Erin with you?"

"No, why? Damon, what's going on?!" Her voice fell an octave.

"She's missing. I think the killer has her."

"What? Are you sure? What should we do?"

"You're going to do nothing. You'll stay and keep the children safe, you and Jonas. I'll find her myself. However, as much as I don't want to, I may have to contact the department to get some backup."

"It's just me tonight. Jonas is working late. But I promise I'll lock up. And Damon, you'll find her. Promise me you will."

"I promise." I hung up.

Corrupted or not, I was sure the department only had one or two bad eggs. A town-wide search would have more good guys looking for Erin than bad ones. It couldn't hurt to call and notify them. They didn't want another murder on their hands; the townspeople were becoming untrusting.

"I need to speak with the chief. This is Damon Clark. It's urgent," I commanded, power in my voice.

I had to utilize every emotional skill they taught us in the Navy because I could feel myself quickly spiraling out of control. If there was anything I would never forget, it's that losing control of your emotions meant losing control of yourself. You made irrational decisions, and you made mistakes.

"Hi, Damon. They said it was urgent," the chief said on the phone.

"You need to issue a search. Erin Summers is the latest target of our serial killer. He's kidnapped her from work today, and he has her now."

"How can you be sure?"

"I have her text messages. There's footage of her leaving our workplace in a red sedan today. License plate is ZX10R73."

"I believe you. I'll look that up right now and see if we can pull a name."

There were two minutes of silence while he did a quick vehicle search, and I was chomping at the bit the entire time.

"Damon? You still there?"

"I'm here. What did you find?"

"The car was registered to Anne Edwards. Her son Jamie Edwards is a desk officer with our department." He sounded confused.

Bingo. But a desk officer surely didn't orchestrate all of this.

"He's a rat, but I don't think he's the killer. He's got to

be working for him. Just like your other officer who was shot. Is there someone above him who he gravitated towards? We have to find the boss. He's the one who has Erin." My voice was firm and unwavering.

"I'm issuing a search right now. We will find her, I promise."

"Thank you. I'll be in touch."

Before I could spiral, I jumped into my car and sped home. There would be people looking for her. That was all I could hope for. But it didn't mean I was going to sit back on my ass. I had a set of skills as well. If anyone stood a chance of finding her, it was me.

Unlocking my gun safe when I arrived home, I armed myself with two handguns, stowing one in my ankle band and another in the belt of my pants. I slid a pocket knife into my inner jacket pocket and grabbed my keys. The guy had a theme with industrial areas, or at least his minions did. My plan was to hit all the industrial buildings in town, both current and abandoned. It would likely take me all night and well into the morning.

I didn't care, though.

The first stop on my Erin search tour took me to the Locke door knob and key factory. They were still in business, and a few employees filed in and out as they shut down for the day. The owner, Sebastian Locke, was a good friend of mine. He was leaning outside, smoking a cigarette as he stared mindlessly at his phone. He didn't even see me walk up.

"Do you let your employees do this?" I half-joked.

"Damon. My man. What brought you over to this side of town?"

"A favor. You haven't seen anyone suspicious around this factory today, have you? It may even be a worker, though I doubt it."

"No, I'm sorry. What is this about?" Sebastian eyed me, but then they flickered to his phone as he got a text message.

"Search for Erin Summers? She's missing?" He seemed perplexed.

"Let me see that." I grabbed his phone, reading the screen.

Sure enough, he was telling me the truth. The police department had issued a town-wide warning to join in on the search.

Immediately, my phone started ringing. First, with a call from my sister. Then, Ellison.

Shit. Ellison. He was the one person I didn't call.

"Hi." I didn't know what else to say.

"My sister is missing? You were supposed to protect her!" He was furious.

"I did. I didn't let her out of my sight except at work. He texted her, and she willingly left."

"Why in the world would my idiotic sister do that?"

"To protect you, Ellison. To protect your mom and dad, too. He was threatening to hurt you all."

"What a… I'm going to wring my little sister's neck when I see her… because we *are* going to see her again. What's your plan? I know you have one."

I filled him in on my search and the weapons I brought. Locke's was a bust. Thankfully, I had another dozen spots to hit.

The sky had begun to darken by the time I searched the fifth location. Eventually, I reached the one industrial building where I witnessed a murder only days prior. It was scrubbed clean. Besides the newly polished floor, there was nothing out of place there. On the way out, I noticed an envelope taped to the wall that I missed on the way in.

As I opened it, I could see a neatly folded paper inside. It had *Damon* written on the outside.

You won't find her. But happy looking.

Now he was taunting me. I was fuming. Something about this was off. He didn't do this with the other victims. Erin was different.

Maybe he likes her.

And, therefore, would have a vendetta against me. This is a game to him. And he thinks he's winning.

As I crumpled the note and shoved it in my pocket, I checked this place off the list. The fact that the note was here meant that the killer knew I was going to be looking in industrial sites to find her. He was smart and trying to think one or two steps ahead. The purpose of the note was not only to antagonize me but to throw me off my trail… get me to look elsewhere. I would be doing no such thing.

"Damon!" Ellison shouted my name from the distance as I approached my truck.

"What are you doing here?"

"I'm helping you. She's my sister, and nobody is going to hurt her. I thought you could use a little backup." He climbed into my passenger seat.

I guess there's no use in trying to object.

We drove around, hitting every other spot on my list except for one. My stomach was grumbling in protest, and my eyes felt dry and irritated.

It didn't matter.

Nothing without her mattered.

"I still have one more spot on my list. I can drop you off," I offered, but Ellison shook his head.

He was in this for the long haul.

"Alright, it's a few minutes away. Let's go."

Once we arrived, Ellison approached the left side of the building while I circled around the right. There was the distinct sound of mumblings inside. It could very well be squatters, or it was my girlfriend being terrorized by a madman.

I peered in one of the downstairs windows. It was empty. But as I slid inside, I heard two shots go off outside, followed by Ellison's screams of agony.

No. No, no, no.

"Ellison!" I screamed, running around to him with my weapon drawn, ready to attack.

"Damon!" I heard Erin's scream as the same red sedan I had seen earlier on the security footage drove off in the distance.

I need to chase them. But if I left Ellison here, he was sure to die. The bullets looked to have grazed his heart, and he had a lot of bleeding.

It was precisely the plan. If I chased Erin and left her brother here, and he died and she lived, then she would be furious with me. Not only that, but I never left a brother behind.

"Let's go, I got you. The hospital is ten minutes away." I lifted Ellison by his arms, straddling him on my back.

"Go after her…" he groaned.

"No. You'll die. I can't leave you behind. I will find her again."

I dialed the hospital as I drove twenty miles over the speed limit.

"We have a gunshot victim coming right now!" I shouted.

Just a few minutes later, I was pulling into the parking lot, where nurses and doctors pulled him out of the car and began to wheel him inside.

"Go, Damon! I'm okay. Go save my sister," he commanded before he was wheeled in and out of my sight.

I will.

Chapter Twenty-One

ERIN

Two days. It had been two days without a shower, without a decent meal, and without Damon. I had no doubt he was looking for me, but we'd moved right after the shots rang out.

I tearfully coaxed a confession out of Jonas, who promised that he had spared Damon. However, he had shot my brother. The news alone sent me to my knees mentally. I wouldn't let him see me crack, though.

I was forced to listen to him call Cara for the past few days, each time with a new excuse for why he couldn't come home. The most recent one was that it was an impromptu work trip, and that he would miss her.

He was having a lot of fun with me, as he liked to remind me often.

My days were spent tied to various pieces of furniture as Jonas alternated between verbally abusing me and proclaiming his love.

"Did you bring me here to kill me? Then do it. Kill me," I said one day, which raised a brow.

Reverse psychology. Let's see if it works.

"Kill you? Now, why would I do that? We're having so much fun," he smiled, returning to his cooking.

We were in a remote cabin, the location unknown to me. I thought I knew his plan—kill me and move on. But here he was, hanging onto me like I was a suitcase full of money he found.

Then, it hit me as I stared at the floor in frustration. Wood made up ninety-five percent of this cabin, and I suddenly remembered a fact from the police reports Damon had shown me—the women all had wood splintering under their nails. He had taken me to his kill site, but it was clear he wanted to take his sweet time. There was something else at play here.

"Then, what's the plan here? You do have to go home eventually to your kids… to your wife. Are you dragging it out long enough to pull suspicion to yourself?" I gaslighted, hoping it was enough to help him change his mind.

It wouldn't be. Guys like Jonas operated on one thing only: the pleasure they got from being in control.

"No. Are you hungry?" He leaned the pan down, showcasing his disgusting dinner.

Over the course of our time together, I had learned that Jonas was a creature of habit, and his favorite meal to eat was mashed potatoes and grilled chicken. It was awfully bland, and yet he grossly lapped it up like it was a five-star meal.

"Not eating again?" He eyed me as he took a seat next to me at the dining table.

My hands and feet were fastened to the dining table chair, so I couldn't feed myself if I tried. Jonas didn't mind;

he loved trying to feed me. The action made my stomach curdle, and the sight of his food didn't look too hot either, so I had been refusing altogether. But now I was starting to feel weak from the missed meals, and it wasn't really smart, given that I would need to fight back.

The problem was that I had no idea where we were.

"Actually, it looks pretty good…" I offered, cringing at the way my voice came out.

Anger wasn't working with him. Defiance was a bust. The only thing that would work to my advantage with Jonas would be to play along with whatever sinister game I found myself trapped in. For whatever reason, killing me wasn't satisfying enough for him. He wanted to play a long game.

"Really? I'm so glad to hear that." Jonas pushed the plate towards me.

Instantly, I was brought back to my dinner at his house, where I sat beside my best friend, him, and their two beautiful children. He was so normal, albeit a little standoffish from time to time. I knew him growing up, and he always made my friend happy. That's all I needed to know.

Now, I wish I'd dug a little deeper. When all this was over, my friend was going to lose out on her husband, who she had been with since high school. Her kids were going to lose their father, one way or another. If Damon didn't kill him for what he did to me, then he would be in jail for the rest of his life. They would throw the book at him.

He offered me a small bite. It wasn't bad, surprisingly. Jonas, on the other hand, was moaning in delight like he had never had something so delicious.

Get me out of here.

He had fastened my arms tightly to the chair along with my legs. I could barely move, let alone get out and escape. Jonas had me secured for the entirety of the day, and he kept bells at the tips of the door frames and handles. I wouldn't be able to move without waking him, even if he were asleep.

"So tell me, why Damon?"

What does that mean?

"Why not him? He's a wonderful man." I didn't want to say more for fear of sparking his temper, which seemed to turn on a dime.

"You never were into him when we were in high school…" He placed another bite in his mouth.

"The age difference back then was weird. Besides, he had no interest in me then. I was awkward and dorky."

"I noticed you. I had interest. I always have," he said, his eyes not leaving mine.

Yeah, right. You married my best friend. He's losing his mind.

"You've been with Cara since high school. This doesn't make any sense."

"I buried my feelings for a long time because I did love her. It didn't feel right to throw it away for something I *could* have had. But keeping my feelings buried for so long… it was impossible. I'm not sure what made me snap that day in particular…"

That's when the murders started.

"Your first kill."

"The one and only. She didn't even see it coming. My hands wrapped around her throat so quickly, and she was powerless. That feeling of watching the light go out of her eyes—it wasn't like anything I had ever felt before. It was euphoric. I couldn't stop… then you came to town. It was harder to keep myself under control. From that point forward, you were the target." His hands moved around with excitement as he told me his story.

"And I'm your final kill… huh?" My gut clenched in

fear as I asked the question I wasn't sure I wanted the answer to.

"No, Erin. You're not." He stood and dumped his empty plate in the sink.

Jonas walked away before I could get another word in. He left me to sit, half of my plate still waiting to be eaten.

"Hello? Did you forget that I don't have access to my hands?" I shouted as I could hear Jonas rattling around in the other room.

He stormed in, quickly fed me the rest of my food, and pulled my chair into the bedroom. Jonas unclipped one limb at a time, reclipping them to the bed frame so I had no chance at escape.

"Where are you going?" I pressed.

"Cara is asking too many questions. I have to go back for the night, probably tomorrow morning. I'll be back soon, my love." He rubbed the top of my head.

I tried not to cringe.

I'm getting the fuck out of here.

I waited until the door closed and I could hear his car pull away from the cabin before I started vigorously yanking on the bed frame. The clanking noise of the handcuffs was loud. Undoubtedly, he received them from one of his crooked buddies on the police force. One thing I knew for sure was that there were always two copies of a key. That ensured that someone couldn't be stuck in a pair forever.

This is useless.

I made no progress shaking the bed frame. Instead, I decided to try something different. Gripping both hands on the top of the frame, I used my feet to kick the bottom as hard as I could. As a result, there was an intense pull on my legs with every down thrust. The bed started to quiver slightly but still didn't budge.

Keys. Find the keys.

I wasn't able to search with my hands or feet, so that was another bust. My body was growing more and more frustrated with the lack of mobility. Keeping myself composed and preventing myself from showing any sign of weakness around Jonas was much more challenging as I grew more stressed. He would mentally break me through the restricted use of my limbs, keeping me bedridden, only allowing me to eat when he fed me...

And then I saw the key hanging from the bedpost on a chain. He must have left it there after locking me up this morning. He did seem distracted.

No fucking way.

Turning on my side, I leaned my head down as far as I could to take the key in between my teeth. My neck started to scream in pain before I finally got it, and then yanked quickly to break the chain. I spit the key to the sheets, then took it in my mouth again and sat up to unlock my right hand.

Once I freed my one hand, I could move quickly to free the rest of myself. My ankles and wrists ached to the touch and were purple from the indents of the cold metal cuffs.

I had no idea how far Jonas had gone or when he would return. He said it would be at least a night and a morning. However, it became increasingly clear that he liked to mess with my head, so I could not believe him.

I started to search the house for something—anything. There were no landlines, and he appeared to have taken his cell phone with him. There was no way to call for help or let anyone know where I was.

I stepped outside, and sure enough, I could see only trees for miles. If I wanted to venture it on foot, I could end up lost with no way out. A quick look around the property brought me face to face with my saving grace—a run-down car.

I need to find the keys.

As I ran back inside, I didn't see any hanging on the hooks. The drawers were dusty and filled with old envelopes and documents. In the top left-hand corner, I saw the cabin address.

Anderson Clark
238 Davenport Road

This was Cara and Damon's parents' cabin. I had never been before, but it looked like it hadn't been used in years. The keys had to be around here somewhere. There was no way their dad left a car with no keys in the garage. He hated having clutter.

Anderson's tackle box sat on top of the fridge.

It's worth a try. He loves to fish more than anything.

Inside was one single car ignition key, paired with a different shaped key, likely to open the door.

Please work.

The engine roared to life underneath me as I stuck the key in the ignition. I nearly cried from gratefulness. I can do this. I could save myself. It was beginning to darken in the sky, and I knew it was now or never. The car creaked and moaned in protest as I quickly gassed it out of the garage.

I started down the road in no particular direction. Even if I was heading the wrong way, I knew it would find town in no time. I could alert someone there.

The car was making great time until I approached a slow vehicle in front of me. They were going way under any speed limit and continuously slammed on their breaks. I had to swerve the car multiple times to avoid colliding with them. By the third instance, it had raised red flags.

Something was wrong.

Chapter Twenty-Two

DAMON

In all my years, I had never felt this way before. I had years of training, tests, and being pushed to my limits, ultimately giving me the strength of durability. That durability was fruitless when the woman that I loved was missing. She was being held by a killer who had been one step ahead this entire time.

When I returned to the building where Ellison had been shot only an hour before, I was both unsurprised and devasted to find that Erin was gone. He had moved her quickly, not wanting to get caught.

They could be anywhere at this point. He wasn't stupid, so he must have driven the second we left and gotten far out of Dodge. What struck me as odd was that he was going to all these lengths. His usual killing style was quick, impulsive, and didn't drag out.

Even so, the fact that he had Erin for nearly two days

now was gut-wrenching. He was straying far from his pattern. He was creating a new one entirely.

Unless she's dead.

The thought was too much to bear. I had been searching for her since I saw she was gone, and I felt no closer to finding her. I had been questioned by the police and given my statement half a dozen times. Ellison was in the hospital but recovering quickly. My sister and Erin's parents were an absolute wreck over it.

As selfish and out of touch as it sounded, I still felt I was in worse shape than any of them, even Ellison. It felt like psychological torture, knowing she was out there somewhere and that I couldn't help her regardless of everything I was doing.

The police assured me that they would bring her in safely. Andrew had been released once they realized what he was saying may actually have some merit. He was also set on finding Erin, although his reasons were likely entirely selfish. Still, I figured it best to use his obsessions with my girlfriend to my advantage. It couldn't hurt to have more hands on deck.

It couldn't just be about the chase. The killer wouldn't be keeping Erin for this long simply because he was scared of being caught. Other factors were at play here, and I racked my brain for days trying to figure out his motives. I figured that if I could figure out his reason for doing this, for straying from his pattern, I would have him right where I wanted him, and Erin would be safe.

I fiddled with my dog tags as I sat on my porch, lost in thought, when it hit me.

It wasn't about those other women. It never was. Erin was the target this entire time. That was the reason that she was kidnapped and not immediately murdered. He had another plan for her. As grateful as I felt in the moment knowing that she was surely alive, I was also absolutely terrified, knowing I still didn't know what that plan entailed.

I had searched over five miles out of town, but I would extend my search today. Andrew insisted on taking a car and helping, so I couldn't refuse. Erin's father was also on the case, incredibly persistent in doing everything he could to bring his little girl home. Ellison also wanted to help, but his mom convinced him to get the rest he needed, and he could help when she was brought home.

Thank God for mothers.

"You heading out now?" Erin's dad called to me from his front door.

"Yeah. I have the car packed. You too?" I eyed my back seat, which had half a dozen legal weapons.

If I found Erin, I wasn't letting her get away without a fight.

"Yessir. Look, I wanted to talk to you for a moment," he said as he approached me.

This could go one of a million ways.

"I know I was against your relationship with my daughter… for a couple of reasons that seem pointless now. I can see, though, through the way that you have been searching for her tirelessly, that you are really good for Erin. I wanted to thank you… and apologize for before." He reached out and squeezed my shoulder.

"No apology necessary. I just want her home, but thank you for that."

"Alright, son. Let's go get our girl." He waved me off as he loaded into his car.

Andrew sent me a text as I barreled down the road, letting me know that he, too, was on his way.

Not only had I been hitting industrial buildings in case the killer struck true to his word, but I had been going door to door with pictures of Erin. One by one, house by house, people assured me they had never seen her and wished me good luck. A few prayed for her. Andrew was in charge of papering the same posters around the area we checked in, just in case someone spotted her. We had no such luck as of yet.

I am going to find you, baby.

As I entered the town of Bransville, I continued where I left off. The first ten doors didn't answer, and the eleventh screamed at me to stop soliciting before I could ask them anything.

Slipping a flier on the porch, I turned to see a neighbor across the street eying me warily.

I'm not a solicitor.

I started to head for them, when they turned on their heel and ran into the house. The door slammed behind them.

What the hell are you hiding?

As I knocked on the door, a face peeked out from the window to the right of it. It was a little girl with freckles and chestnut brown hair who couldn't have been more than seven.

"Hi…" She opened the door cautiously.

"Hi, sweetheart. Is your mom or dad home?" I asked, knowing I had seen a middle-aged woman duck into the house only seconds prior.

She didn't answer, but nodded her head slowly.

"Can I talk to them?"

"Mama doesn't talk to the police," she said matter-of-factly.

"Oh, I'm not the police. I just want to know if you've seen this girl." I held up the picture of Erin, and her body stilled as her little face flashed with recognition.

She slowly nodded before a large hand grabbed the

door and opened it wide.

With a pinched look, the woman scolded her young daughter.

"Amber, I told you never to open the door without me. Please, no soliciting. And for your information, we don't talk to police around here." The woman slammed the door in my face.

She had seen Erin. I was close.

I banged on the door again. Once more, it swung open, but the girl was gone. Her mother appeared furious.

"Look, all you law people think you can do whatever you want. But I have a right not to let you in."

"Ma'am, I'm not police. I'm just looking for this girl. Your daughter said she had seen her." I held up the picture.

She didn't so much as flinch when she saw the photo.

"We ain't seen her around here, and my daughter certainly has not. She doesn't go anywhere. Now, you better get off my property." And once more, the door was shut in my face.

I jotted down the address in my phone as I texted Erin's dad and Andrew.

Damon: I got a lead at this address. Little girl confirms she saw Erin. Mom won't say much. Don't come back here yet. We don't want to be slapped with a harassment charge. Will continue with the neighbors.

Andrew: Will do.

There was no response from her dad, but that wasn't unusual for him. A quick "like" of my message, and I knew he had seen it.

I stayed in the neighborhood, continuing my routine of knocking on doors one by one. The ones who didn't answer received a flyer, and the ones who did told me they had never seen her before.

Either they were lying, or the little girl was, which I doubted. Maybe she was the only one to see Erin, but why? And where? As I knocked on the final door, I saw the mom get in her car and speed off.

There was no sign of the daughter with her.

No better time than now.

I sprinted over and knocked once more. The daughter opened the door and smiled once she saw me.

"Hi! My momma said not to talk to you," she sighed.

"I know, I'm sorry. I won't say anything, but I just wanted to know where you saw that girl. You know, this one?" I held the picture up once more.

She took it in her fingers and then looked incredibly sad.

"She was with a man. He looked really mean. They were at the gas station when I was in the car. She smiled at me."

"Did you see which way they went?"

"Up the big hill." She pointed to the long road that led to the cabin areas.

I knew that most of them were uninhabited during this time of year. They usually served as vacation homes.

I guess that's all I would get out of her. It wasn't super promising, but it was a lead. Maybe Erin was in the immediate area.

Or he took her and used the gas to go even farther.

He had to return at some point, didn't he? If he lived in town, he would definitely have a job. A job would be missing him, surely. He had bills and things to pay for. Of course, he could also be someone who still lived with his parents and never worked a day in his life.

At this point, I couldn't be sure of anything. I texted Erin's dad and Andrew.

Damon: I talked to the girl. She said she saw Erin and some man at the gas station- he looked mean- and Erin smiled at her.

Not much to go on, but at least we know we're looking in the right area.

I went through three neighborhoods before calling in for a break and grabbing lunch. Her father had hit two, and Andrew had done three as well. The next area was the cabins. I had one in the area about a twenty-minute drive away, and my parents had one down the road from mine.

It couldn't hurt to check for squatters, in any case.

"How did you boys fare?" I took a bite of my hamburger.

"Not that good. Nobody has seen her, which checks out with the idea that they traveled in the nighttime. Also, a lot of people were upset that we were knocking on their door so early," Andrew mumbled.

If you ever told me I would be sharing a meal with this guy, I would have laughed in your face.

"Same here. I gave out lots of flyers, though. We'll find her, I promise."

The burger tasted like dirt in my mouth. All I could think of was her—where she was, what she was doing, if she was okay.

She was kidnapped. I knew deep down she was far from okay. Maybe it was worth calling the police chief to check if anyone hadn't reported in for work the past few days. Exploring every single avenue would be the way to ensure her return home.

I quickly put down the rest of my food and got right back out there. I wouldn't relax for too long. Every minute I waited was another minute of her life being in this psycho's hands. I needed to focus on finding these cabins on these unmarked wooded roads.

"Holy shit." My mouth went dry as a terrifying realization hit me.

This is where he has her. The wood under the victims'

nails suddenly made sense—these old cabin floors and walls. Had they been trapped, and clawing to escape?

But why here? Maybe he owned property in this area. However, we knew a lot of the neighbors. Most were older couples or young families. Or this person knew that they were mostly vacant and seized that opportunity to use someone's home as their private torture spot.

My family's cabin was the first on the route, and as I pulled into the driveway, there was a fresh set of tire tracks. A car had been here recently.

I stuck my handgun into my waistband and slowly approached the house.

Chapter Twenty-Three

ERIN

I tried to swerve the car, slam on the brakes, anything. This car was actively going out of its way to make me crash into them—and I could do nothing about it. It was a one-way road, and there was no way to turn around. My stomach churned, and I had a bad feeling.

Finally, I stopped the car completely, testing a theory. The car in front of me abruptly stopped and started to back up.

Shit.

I did as well, and they started to speed up. I couldn't get away fast enough. Our cars collided, and I was jolted back in my seat when the steering wheel airbag smacked me in the face. I was knocked unconscious.

As I slowly peeled open my eyes, I rubbed my sore neck.

What happened?

Everything slowly flooded back. My heartbeat started

to thump out of my chest as my vision cleared. I was handcuffed to a metal chair in a home I didn't recognize. He had moved me from the cabin.

He's growing desperate. This has to end soon.

"Good morning, sleepyhead. I have to admit, your escape attempt was brave… but misguided. We were having so much fun. Why would you want to leave?" Jonas cooed. I saw scratches on his face, likely from the car accident he caused.

"Why would I want to be stuck here? You're my best friend's husband. This is wrong, and you know it!" I wailed.

Honesty seemed like a good idea at this point. Jonas had always been charming, and he wasn't shy about his good looks. But yet, he was the classic wolf in sheep's clothing. He had fabricated an entire connection between us, and maybe a little raw honesty would bring him back to reality.

My escape attempt failed. He was two steps ahead, and for some reason, he had no intention of letting me go. I had become his plaything, and he felt like he owned me… owned my life.

"My prisoner? Erin… you're going to be my wife." He smiled, placing his hand on mine.

You have a wife.

"What? What about Cara? You have a family. I don't want to be your wife," I spat.

His face pinched up in anger. Jonas's eyes went dark and cold as he stood up, punching a hole in the wall.

"Now, that doesn't sound very grateful, Erin. I could have easily killed you like the others. But you're special. It's a lot to swallow, but you'll see. We'll be happy here." He motioned to the small kitchen we sat in.

The place was run-down and seemed abandoned. He was clearly deep in his delusion, and anything I said to him wouldn't pull him out of it. In fact, it was more likely than anything to anger him more and increase the likelihood of him snapping and doing something he would later regret.

Something like killing me. No, I had to play this smart.

"Wow, the house is nice. Can I get a tour?"

"I don't know if I can trust you." His eyes scanned me, unsure of my motives.

Don't oversell it.

"Fine, then don't. I just thought it would be nice to see where we were going to live." I looked to the side defiantly.

"Okay, fine. But just for a few minutes."

Jonas uncuffed both of my hands, then double-cuffed them back together, binding me at the ankles and my elbows behind my back.

Extra security, great.

"So this is the kitchen," he said as he gestured to the room around us. The tile was partially broken, falling from the wall, and the linoleum was peeling. Wallpaper was pulled off in sections around us, and the faded wooden cabinets were less than appealing.

Are you really being picky about your fake house, Erin?

"This is the living room, the bathroom, and this… will be our bedroom. As you can see, I'm working on this room first." Jonas led me to a small bedroom with paint cans on the floor.

He thinks we're just going to leave everything, everyone behind and start new together. He's truly lost it.

"It looks great," I lied.

"Hmm. Are you hungry? I was just about to make something?"

I nodded, and he brought me back to the chair in the kitchen, securing me once more. Jonas turned away and started assembling something to eat. Sweat formed on my face, and I so badly wanted to wipe it away.

Stolen From My Billionaire Boss

"So, how did everything go?"

He turned around, confused.

"I don't know what you mean."

"When you went back. Did Cara suspect anything?"

"I didn't make it back. Your little escape attempt kept me from doing that. It's safe to say she's very upset and a little worried. Nevertheless, it won't matter soon enough." He moved sautéed veggies around a pan nonchalantly.

What does that mean? I'm scared to ask and find out.

"God, that cut looks bad. I'll have to get you bandaged up." He dabbed at my forehead with a paper towel.

Not sweat… blood. I was bleeding.

"Maybe I should get to a doctor?"

"No." He didn't think twice about the answer.

I was all out of questions; frankly, I think he was tired of answering them. So we sat silently as he cooked what was likely some bland chicken dish again. My mind was only on one thing, one person—Damon. He must be going out of his mind with worry. I have no doubt my family was doing everything they could.

My brother had been shot, and I was given no news, no update on if he was okay. I couldn't stand the thought of him being seriously hurt, and I knew for a fact that it was the last possible thing Jonas worried about. Otherwise, he wouldn't have shot him in the first place.

"Bon appetit." Jonas set a place in front of me.

"Meatballs… they look delicious, thank you," I complimented.

His eyebrows raised in surprise. He expected defiant and angry Erin, but I knew that wasn't working with him. Instead, he would get pleasant and compliant Erin. It was the only way to placate him enough to give me some freedom.

"Could I have a little room to eat?" I pulled on one of the handcuffs.

Please don't feed me again.

"Okay, but if you try and do something, they will be going back on." He pulled the key from his pocket.

I doubt he would be hiding it near the bed anytime soon.

"I won't, promise."

As promised, the cuffs came off on one hand, and I was able to feed myself the surprisingly decent lunch. Who knew he could cook something other than chicken after all?

I was scared, but the fear was less than it was a few days prior. Jonas made it very clear that he didn't want to hurt me. He wanted to be with me. As stomach-clenching as that was, it was a good thing. It meant I didn't need to fear my immediate death unless I continued to be a problem for him.

So I had two options: wait to be rescued or do it myself. Either way, both plans included me being docile and sweet enough to keep Jonas along for the ride.

"You look like you're enjoying it," he murmured, appreciatedly.

"It's amazing. I was starving," I laughed.

His eyes settled on me, blazing deep.

How long would it be before he tried something? Jonas was infatuated with me, and he wanted a life together. If Cara was any indication, it meant he wanted kids and a wife. I couldn't give him either of those things, but I could sure as hell make him believe I would. It was the only way out.

We sat in silence for the rest of the meal, with Jonas casting occasional glances my way. I couldn't be sure if he believed the docile act I was giving him or was just going along with it.

"What are you going to do about Cara?" I asked as he collected the plates.

Jonas stopped abruptly at the sink, his back tightening under his t-shirt.

Oh shit, did I overstep?

"I'm going to get rid of her," he said, emotionless.

"What do you mean by that?" My stomach tightened with anxiety.

"It's nothing you need to worry about. But she would definitely make waves for us, a lot of trouble."

Oh god, no. He plans to kill her.

"And your kids?"

"They can live with their grandparents. They also joked about wanting to." He giggled as if it were the funniest thing in the world.

Kill your wife and abandon your children. And this man thinks I should jump into life with him. Get me the fuck out of here. I have to warn Cara somehow.

"Ah, I see. Makes sense. So... what do we do about the lack of furniture in here?" I changed the subject.

His mood lightened instantly, and a smile spread across his face.

"I was thinking we could get the laptop and look online today. Maybe do some online shopping and pick out some pieces. What do you think?"

"That sounds good."

He was buying it, my enthusiasm. I didn't need to sell it as much as I thought I would. Jonas was truly a psychopath. His superficial charm had helped him coast through life this far, and now he was confident that it had won me over.

He washed the dishes as I lightly tugged on all my

restraints. As expected, none of them were giving even slightly. Jonas didn't turn once. He was in his own world, humming some old tune.

He planned to kill my best friend. She had no idea what was coming, and I had no way to warn her. But I had to figure something out, and quickly. I couldn't let her die, especially if there were something I could do to stop it.

Jonas pulled out the laptop when he finished and uncuffed me so we could go on the couch. He left both my hands and legs free and had me sit down next to him.

I could run. Right here, right now.

But that was stupid. I needed to bide my time, or I don't think he would ever believe my docile act again.

"Where should we look? Living Spaces?" He smiled, typing into the browser.

An array of online furniture flooded the screen and he slowly scrolled, selecting bedroom furniture first.

Dear god.

I pretended to be excited about armoires while I ran through how he was able to access the site. Having internet meant having access to the outside world. I could send a message to Cara or Damon telling them where I was…

The question was how to do it without Jonas noticing. I figured I could try when he was asleep, but he would likely have me cuffed. Maybe I could drug him, but then again, the limited use of my hands and legs wasn't working to my advantage.

"Erin… did you hear me?" Jonas's voice broke me from my thoughts.

"No, sorry. What did you say?"

"I asked if you liked this bed." He pointed to the screen with a picture of an espresso-colored four-point king bed.

"Sure, that's perfect."

"You don't seem into this. Is everything okay?"

"I think I'm a little tired, honestly. And my wrists are a little sore." I rubbed them, feeling where the indents of the cuffs lay.

His face looked apologetic.

"I suppose I could leave them off. But only if I can trust you."

"You can. I promise. I'm all yours."

The words felt like acid coming out of my mouth, but they pleased Jonas, and that was the only thing I could do at the moment to keep him unsuspecting.

"I'll take a nap with you. I'm a little tired, too. We can pick this up later." He shut the laptop and set it on the table, leading me to the air mattress he had set up temporarily.

Bingo.

Chapter Twenty-Four

DAMON

The cabin was empty, but there were signs of a struggle. One of the bed frame posts had scratches, and a broken chain, like for a necklace or dog tags, lay on the floor.

"Why the hell would the cabin look like this?" I muttered to myself.

I called Cara on my speed dial.

"Damon? Did you find her?"

"Not yet. I'm close, though. I'm not sure if this is related, but someone's been at our mom and dad's cabin. It looks like signs of a struggle. I would say break-in, but nothing was taken besides Dad's old car from the garage."

There was silence on the other line, almost as if she was processing the information in her head.

"Do you think she was there?"

The thought did cross my mind. But why would she be brought here? To my family's cabin? There were plenty of homes in the area. It can't be a coincidence.

"I'm not sure. Why would they come here?" I questioned, hoping she could answer the question that I couldn't.

"Oh my god… I have to go," and my sister hung up abruptly.

It sounded like she'd pieced something together, and she wasn't ready to share it with me. I would give her some time, then call her back. I couldn't be sure if this was related to Erin. Something in my gut told me it was, though.

I pulled out my phone.

Damon: Break in at my parents' cabin. Looks like a struggle. No evidence of Erin, but I have a strong feeling she was here.

Andrew: Anything missing?

Damon: My dad's old car.

Brian: Call the local police department. Report it missing. Hopefully if we track down the car, we track down my daughter.

Damon: Got it.

Brian wasn't much for texting, but he was right. If we registered the car as stolen, it would be a red flag for any officer who ran the plates. With any luck, it was parked somewhere close to where they were hiding, and I could get Erin back.

I felt drained. Sitting at the dining table, I noticed deep scratch marks in the wood. Running my finger along the indents, they felt and looked eerily similar to the ones on the bed frame.

These were from handcuffs, there was no doubt about it. And suddenly, there was no doubt that Erin was here. She was held hostage, right in this very chair. I had hardened to these kinds of things over time due to my line of work, but thinking of her here, bound and scared… well, my stomach was sick, to say the very least.

It truly wasn't a coincidence. Someone took Erin, and

then they felt comfortable enough to take her here. These past few days, it felt personal. I figured it was a grudge against me, perhaps. But maybe the person was just close to us.

And suddenly, Cara's behavior clicked and made sense. She'd figured it out before me.

Jonas had been here many times before. He was comfortable, and he knew where everything was.

I called my sister's phone back, but it went straight to voicemail. I called again, and nothing. I was so close to Erin, I could feel it. But I needed to figure out what my sister knew. Maybe she could help me narrow down where else he would've gone.

I texted Andrew and Brian, letting them know I was going back home to talk to my sister and then I would rejoin them.

As I drove ten miles over the speed limit down the highway, I dialed my sister three times more. Every time, it went to voicemail. Finally, I got an automated text response.

Cara: Can I call you back?

I rolled my eyes.

"No, the fuck you can't!" I yelled at my phone, talking to nobody in particular.

Her house was about thirty minutes away, but I was determined to make it that much quicker. My foot lay on the gas, my truck barreling past cars. A few angry honks were directed my way, but I couldn't muster enough energy to care. Everything I had in me was directed towards finding Erin.

As I pulled into her gravel driveway, I spotted my sister pacing on the porch with a worried look. She was so lost in thought that she didn't look up when I arrived.

"Cara! What's going on?"

Her head snapped up, finally realizing I was there.

"Damon, you shouldn't have come. I'm sorry I didn't answer your calls," she apologized.

Her appearance was disheveled, her clothes dirty and unwashed, her hair unbrushed, and her eyes red from crying.

"Stop. Something I said upset you, and I know you have a good gut feeling about things like this. You can tell me anything. What is it, Cara?"

Tell me. Tell me you think your husband did this.

She sat on her rocking chair, and I joined her in the one opposite her, wiping sweat off my face.

"Jonas. He hasn't been home in a few days. He claims it's work, but I called them, and he has been out sick, apparently."

And there it is.

"Did you two have a fight? You know how he runs off to a hotel sometimes to blow off steam…" I tried to comfort my sister.

Obviously, her failing marriage was that much heavier of a burden, with her best friend missing as well. I wanted to fix things for her… for everyone. Right now, I had tunnel vision, though.

"No, we didn't. Everything was fine. At first, I thought he might be cheating. I came to terms with that possibility. I grieved, I cried. But after I talked to you, something clicked."

"What did?"

"Was the house broken into? Any signs of a broken door, broken windows?"

"No, none. That's what was so odd. What are you getting at?"

"The only person who knew where the key was for the cabin, besides Mom, Dad, me, and you… was Jonas."

And it all comes together.

So many things began to fit into place, but the realization also opened up so many questions. It explained the choice of cabin, why he shot Ellison and not me, and why women were chosen. I know my sister and he had some issues recently. He was cold and distant with her, and it all checked out.

"He took Erin…" I mumbled in a state of shock. I had started to put it together, but my sister confirmed it. Holy shit. He was right in front of my face the entire time, and I didn't see it.

I had a responsibility to my town, but most of all, to my sister, niece, and nephew. I should have kept them safe. Instead, they had a killer living with them. A killer who now went after my girlfriend with some twisted other plan for her.

"My husband is a murderer," she sobbed into my shoulder.

I need to bring the police in on this as soon as possible.

I rubbed my sister's head in comfort. Knowing the killer's identity gave us an edge. He probably thought he was untouchable, and he was sorely mistaken. I excused myself momentarily once Cara pulled herself together and made a conference call.

"Damon, is everything okay with your sister?" Brian asked, concerned.

"We know who the killer is and who has Erin."

"What? Who is it?" Andrew shouted.

"Jonas. Her husband. I'm not sure what the reason is, but we are sure it's him. I'll be alerting the local police force. I was hoping you could do me a favor and call all the stations in the cities and towns we searched. They all need to be looking for him."

"Oh my god. I always treated him so well. I've let him into my home!" Brian yelled, anger clear in his voice.

"I know, I know. I feel the same way, but we only need to focus on finding her right now. The anger can wait."

"You're right," both Brian and Andrew confirmed.

They hung up to start calling the stations as I dialed up our local one.

"This is Damon Clark. I need to speak with the chief," I commanded.

"One second, please…" and the hold music flooded the phone.

"Damon, any news? We've been looking, but there's not much of a trail left."

"The killer is my sister's husband, Jonas."

"Are you sure? He's a respected member of this community," disbelief clear in his voice.

"I'm sure. And he's hardly that. He's a murderer, a kidnapper, and he tried to kill Ellison Summers and failed. He has Erin, and I'm going to find her. I thought you should know who it was so you can keep an eye out," and I hung up.

I didn't have time to get into all the nitty gritty details with him. My girl's life was at stake, and I needed to get to her. Jonas and Erin couldn't have gotten far, and I needed to find her.

"Cara, I have to go. Will you be okay here?"

"Yes, go- bring her home," she said tearfully.

I plan to.

My drive was jam-packed with worry. My venture home was necessary, but I couldn't help but feel that I wasted valuable time in finding Erin. Knowing that it was Jonas was all the confirmation I needed to find her. He went to my parents' cabin because it was convenient. He had a key, and he had just shot her brother. Jonas needed a quick getaway, and somewhere nobody would ask questions or recognize him.

Cara said his car was gone. That meant there was no reason for him to take my dad's car from the cabin. So why did he?

Maybe Erin took it. Was she trying to flee?

Did he catch her?

Was she hurt?

This was the most painful couple of days I had ever experienced. It was pure torture knowing that someone you loved was in danger, and everything you were doing may not be enough.

I was willing to bring down heaven and Earth to find her and bring Jonas to justice. Not only would bringing him in bring closure to the families of the women he killed, but also for Erin, my sister, and my niece and nephew. Everyone in this town had been affected by his actions, and there was no shortage of people wanting to see him pay.

I pulled up in front of my own cabin soon after. Brian and Andrew had already searched my parents' cabin, and the police were there now, searching. If there were anything new to find… they would find it.

My cabin was untouched as far as I could see. My phone buzzed with a text from Andrew.

Andrew: Here's a crazy thought. What about houses in the area? Could he be a renter? Maybe Airbnb? There were no hotel rooms under his name or hers.

No, he couldn't be renting unless he had applied and found a place quite some time ago. While possible, it just didn't seem likely to me. No… that couldn't be what was going on. Still, Andrew had a point. Jonas didn't think we were on to him in the slightest. He probably had let his guard down significantly.

If he wasn't in a hotel, an Airbnb, or renting a place

out here, then he was shacked up somewhere… somewhere where they wouldn't ask questions or check your credit score.

He was hiding out somewhere uninhabited, possibly a house for sale or rent that was still vacant. He would need lots of space, likely a big yard, and no close neighbors. I pulled out my iPhone, searching for a list of homes fitting the criteria on Zillow. There were three in the town.

I sent one to Brian and one to Andrew and saved the most likely one for myself. It was hard to put them in situations where they could get hurt, but her dad wouldn't forgive me if I cheated him of the chance of saving his daughter himself.

It's go time.

Chapter Twenty-Five

ERIN

We lay in the bed, facing away from each other as Jonas drifted to sleep. His snoring filled the room, and my heart beat rapidly as I slowly moved out of the bed. One foot came off at a time, and my fingers wiggled slowly, the mattress creaking once before I was on my feet. My eyes scanned Jonas, searching for any sign of movement, but he was out cold.

Sure, kidnapping and murder will tire a guy out.

I tiptoed over to the laptop, opening it slowly. It made a low whirring noise as it powered to life. His home screen prompted me with a password.

Password? Fuck! I didn't see him type a password earlier.

Cara. Try again.
Lila. Try again.
Luke. Try again.
Oh, please, no.
Erin. Access granted.

Sick freak.

I pulled up my social media account and logged in. To the side of me, Jonas shifted on the bed, and my breath hitched in my chest. His hand reached up and rubbed his face in his sleep, but he was unflinching.

Damon's phone was online. I messaged him.

Erin: Damon, it's me. I have access to a computer while he sleeps. I need help.

Damon: Erin-We're looking for you. Where are you?

Erin: Some old, random house. I don't know the address.

Damon: I'm tracking this computer. Stay put.

I logged out, cleared the history, and powered it down before Jonas could wake up and see what I was doing. As the screen went dark, I saw a reflection of a man standing behind me.

No.

"You had me fooled, Erin! You'll never accept me or this beautiful gift of a life I've given you," he spat, his hands around my throat.

No. He was going to kill me now. Jonas had realized that I would never submit to him and go along with his plan.

"Jonas, stop!" I screamed as he threw me straight across the floor.

"You know, I would have given you everything. I was committed to you, to us!! Erin, I was willing to get rid of my wife for you. But you don't want it. You don't want me. And now, I have to get rid of you too. You're a loose end." He stomped towards me.

As he dropped to his knees on the other side of me, his hands went around my throat once more. I gripped him with one hand, desperately trying to relieve the pressure as the air was leaving my lungs. My other hand felt around for something, *anything* possible, to free myself.

There was a beer bottle lying underneath the coffee

table. Quickly thinking, I smashed it and jammed the shard into the side of Jonas's neck. He fell to the side, and I scrambled onto my feet, racing for the door. As I opened it, it slammed closed once more, his bloody hand at the top of the doorframe.

He had removed his shirt and wrapped it around his neck, trying to stop the blood flow.

"Jonas, please. You don't have to do this," I begged, trying to pull on any heartstrings he claimed he had for me. It was a last-ditch effort before fighting for my life.

I was playing to his kind side, not likely that he had one.

"On the contrary, sweetheart. I do have to do this. See, you could have been the answer to all my problems. You could have been the reason for all this madness. Instead, you're another problem, just like the rest of them."

The rest of them? His other victims. They weren't the problem. He was.

"You're the problem, Jonas! You're a sociopathic narcissist," I screeched as my elbow connected with his ribs, sending him stumbling backward.

He fell onto the ground, stunned. His neck was spewing blood from his wound, soaking the shirt he had fastened to it. He didn't have long left, one could deduce.

I grabbed a knife from the kitchen counter and approached him slowly. His eyes fixed on mine, and his hand yanked on my ankle, sending me falling and the knife sliding. Jonas turned onto his side and started to army crawl for it. Once back on my feet, I beat him to it and kicked it, making it fly across the room. He rolled onto his back to catch his breath, and I lunged for the knife.

"What, are you going to kill me, Erin? You don't have it in you." He coughed, red blood streaking his chin.

"There's a lot of things you don't know about me, one

being how resilient I am. But you, Jonas, *you* don't have it in you." Then I drove the knife through his heart, painting my face a deep red.

His body slumped almost instantly, and I rolled to the side. Within seconds, I started to heave and sob as I stared in disbelief at his lifeless body. The door burst open, and Damon stood there, wide-eyed at the bloody floor. His gaze softened when he saw I was okay, and he took me in his arms.

Adrenaline is powerful, and the will to survive is one of the most influential driving factors. Once the dust settles, your heart rate slows, and your gaze focuses, we are forced to take in the sight of what we had to do to survive.

I didn't let myself become another one of his victims. I lived. But I also took away the only father my best friend's children had ever known. Knowing that someone was a horrible human being didn't erase the years of good memories and warm and fuzzy feelings toward them. Today, a family would grieve. And another would celebrate when I returned home.

"Erin, you did it. You're safe," Damon whispered in my ear as we sat in the back of the ambulance, a blanket wrapped around me tightly.

"I think you should get checked at the hospital. You could have worse injuries than you know about. In fact, I insist," the paramedic approached me.

"Do what he says. Can she be transferred to our town's hospital?" Damon inquired.

It was nice that he was doing all the talking for me. I was quite frankly at a loss for words and didn't feel capable of putting together a complete sentence.

"Yes, sir, her injuries don't appear to be life-threatening. We will transfer now." He moved me to the stretcher, and Damon climbed in right beside me, my hand in his.

"You may be more comfortable in your own vehicle, following us to the hospital," the paramedic offered.

Damon shook his head vehemently.

"I'm not leaving her side."

"But—"

"I'm. Not. Leaving. Her. Side. End of story."

And that was that. The paramedic ceded to Damon, and the doors shut as we drove down the road. Damon's phone started to buzz and vibrate with calls and texts. He was typing furiously back and forth when he answered the call.

"Yes, she's here." He smiled, rubbing my hand.

He offered the phone to me and mouthed, "Dad."

"Hi dad…" I croaked.

"Erin, oh my god. My baby. I'm so glad you're okay. Your mother and I… we've been worried sick," my dad sobbed into the phone.

He was never much of a crier, and there was something about hearing your parent cry over your well-being when you weren't sure if you were ever going to hear their voice again that just, well, made someone emotional.

"I know, Dad. I know. I'm okay, and I'm coming home."

"I'll meet you at the hospital. And Erin? I love you."

"I love you too, Dad."

"Happy to hear from you?" Damon grinned as he slid his phone back into his pocket.

"Oh man, it was something. Thank you."

"For what? It was all you."

"I know you didn't stop looking. That was one of the only things that kept me going. That, and keeping Cara safe," I confessed.

"Keeping Cara safe… that's where I failed. I should

have seen what a monster he was. But why did you have to keep her safe? He wouldn't have hurt her."

I nodded, confirming the opposite.

"He planned to kill her. When he realized I wasn't truly lining up to be his next wife, that's when he snapped. I don't think he was going to hurt me until then."

Damon nodded, and his eyes darted back and forth, processing the information.

"Wow. I didn't realize. So, what? He was in love with you?"

I could tell Damon hadn't explored that possibility. Quite honestly, he wasn't sure why Jonas took me at all. The real reason took me by surprise when I heard it. He never gave any indication that would lead me to believe it was an option.

"That's what he claims. Who knows how much of that is real truth and how much is fiction. By the way, a cop named Edwards was in on it. I guess he needed the money, and Jonas made an offer he couldn't refuse.

"We're already on it, Sherlock. Look, I should call everyone. Give me a few minutes." Damon stepped to the side, allowing the paramedic to lower me down as we parked.

My father rushed towards me and nodded to Damon. The two exchanged an unspoken agreement as my dad grabbed my hand in his, walking alongside me as I was being led in. In the waiting room, my mom sat with a box of tissues. She jumped up at the sight of me, but the nurses and doctors asked her to sit.

"We've got her from here, we promise," they assured them and wheeled me back between two double doors.

A handful of doctors and nurses checked me over, and I was diagnosed with nothing more than a slight concussion and bruising on my neck.

They gave me a room for a few hours to keep an eye on the concussion, with a promise to let me go soon.

"Hi, beautiful." Damon came in, holding a bouquet as he kissed my head tenderly.

My dad and mother soon followed, her pushing my brother in a wheelchair.

"Don't tell me you can't walk," I joked.

"I'm so glad you're okay." Ellison smiled, but his eyes were wet with tears.

"Me too."

There was a knock on the door, and Cara entered with Luke in her arms and Lila's hand in hers.

This is the moment I have been dreading.

"Hey Luke, Lila, maybe we should give Mommy and Erin a few minutes, yeah? Take you down to the cafeteria?" Damon intervened, and my parents and brother took the hint as well.

The room was cleared out within a minute, leaving only Cara and I to talk.

"Cara, I'm so sorry." I began to dole out apologies, but she held up her hand to stop me.

"Stop it right now. You were protecting yourself. From what Damon tells me, you were protecting me and my children, too. You're a hero. Jonas, well, I can't lie that it didn't feel like some sort of karmic justice," she said as she sat on the bed.

I was flooded with relief. Worry plagued me and made me convinced that my best friend would hate me. Yet here she was, proclaiming that she stood by my actions.

It was everything I needed at the moment.

"I love you." I grabbed her wrist, and she lay beside me in the bed.

"Ditto, babe."

Chapter Twenty-Six

DAMON

Complete, unfounded relief. I don't think I ever felt more at peace knowing Erin was safe and in bed beside me.

Jonas was dead, and my girl was safe.

As relieved as Erin was to be safe and home, she felt enormous guilt, and I could see it clearly on her face. My sister gave her the all-clear in terms of responsibility, but she still had it. She was a good person, unlike Jonas. He killed and killed and then resorted to kidnapping. I think he met a gentler ending than he deserved. Erin, on the other hand, would've preferred anything other than his death at her hands.

The police had interviewed her for hours on end, forcing her to relive everything over and over, and she was deep in sleep next to me.

Erin was right. The police found a notebook with detailed information about everything, which indicted two officers as his running men. Jonas also took it upon himself to journal some of his ramblings, and from what they told us, it was clear he wasn't mentally well. For me, that was a given. His obsession with Erin spanned many years back, dating to when they were in high school. One crush spiraled into the murders of nearly half a dozen innocent women.

And Erin had taken a life, which wasn't sitting easy with her in the slightest. As much as she recognized that it was her only option, it was a real struggle for her.

I couldn't sleep. I don't think I would be able to sleep for a while. I was so grateful to have her back, and I couldn't take my eyes off her.

I wasn't sure I ever wanted to take my eyes off of her again. Realizing that sleep wasn't in my immediate future, I carefully climbed out of bed and took out my phone.

There was only one jeweler in town, and he just so happened to be a very good buddy of mine.

Hopefully, Emilio was awake.

"Hello? Do you know what time it is?" Emilio laughed into the phone.

I knew his ass would be up. He was a certified night owl.

"Hey, man. Would you, by any chance, be in the store?"

"Yes, sir. I'm just about to close up. It's been a busy day. What can I do for you?"

"I need… well, I need a ring."

He laughed. "I think I understand. I can help you out. Want to come in today?"

I checked the time. It had hit one thirty in the early hours of the morning.

"Yes, I'll be there. Thanks, Emilio."

"Hey, Damon… how is she? Your girl," his voice was laced with concern.

"She'll get there. Thanks, man, again. See you later."

"Damon?" Erin's voice sleepily called from the bedroom.

I ran to the room.

"Is everything okay, babe?" My brows furrowed with worry, but she looked fine.

In fact, she looked better than fine.

"Where were you? I got scared."

"I couldn't sleep. I was just hanging out on the couch." I sat next to her and ran my thumb across her sweat-beaded forehead.

"Come here." She snuggled into my chest, and my cock stirred.

It had been too long without her touch, without the smell of her beside me. Erin's eyes cast up to me, dark with lust and desire as she scanned my body.

The curve of her body pressed into me as she leaned in closer, her lips hovering an inch above mine. She looked up, a smirk curving at the edge of her lip.

Oh, she's teasing me.

"What do you want, baby?"

"I want you. I need you." Erin's finger traced circles on my chest seductively.

Grabbing her ass, I flipped her over, so she was on her back, pressed into me. I started planting soft kisses on her collarbone, leading down to below her belly button. She arched in pleasure as a soft moan escaped her lips. Her eyes were hungry, needing.

Erin's hand found my hair as she tugged hard.

"Patience, baby…"

My tongue devoured her slowly, her legs tightening around my head. Her body kept scooting up, the pleasure building higher and higher as she gripped the sheets to steady herself.

"No, wait, Damon. I need to taste you," she begged through metered breaths.

She sat up, pulling my sweatpants down as she took me in her mouth. My hips flexed and tightened as she slowly licked up and down my shaft, my toes curling in response. Her eyes flicked up to mine, gaze intense and unwavering.

"You're so hot, baby. I love when you suck my cock," I groaned.

My words were like fire to her as she accelerated her pace, pumping with one hand as the other found my balls. Her tongue swirled around the tip, and I could feel myself quickly becoming undone.

"Enough, I need to be inside you," I commanded, desperately trying to keep myself from falling over the edge.

She leaned back on the bed as I hovered over her entrance, thrusting in one swift move. Erin's legs wrapped around my back as her fingernails dug into my skin, a stinging sensation burning my back.

"You feel so good, Damon," she moaned in my ear as she bit softly.

Oh god, I could do this forever.

Her body clung to mine like she was scared I'd leave as I continued my pace, feeling her tighten around me.

"Harder, don't stop!"

My rhythm picked up until I was pounding in and out of her. As I leaned down, our mouths found each other, our teeth crashing as our tongues swirled in passion.

This is heaven.

"You feel so good," I growled, feeling close to my edge.

"Damon, I'm close," Erin moaned, her head tipping back.

Oh, I know, baby.

I spilled into her as she met her release, our bodies tensing together before collapsing in ecstasy.

I never want to stop doing this.

"I needed that," I laughed as I pulled her into me, spooning her.

"Me too. I feel a lot better. Let's spend the whole day together," she laced her fingers with mine.

Shit.

"Yes, let's do that. I have a little town business to sort out, so maybe visiting with Cara or your parents is a good idea?" I offered.

Her eyes cast down in disappointment. The last thing I wanted to do was disappoint her, but I couldn't have her come with me to the jewelry shop. It would ruin the surprise of her gift, and I didn't want that.

Sorry, baby. I'll make it up to you soon enough.

"I guess that's fine," Erin sighed.

"Hey, I wanted to talk to you. I know I had you move in under the guise of keeping you safe while the murderer was out. The threat is over, but I don't want you to leave. I was thinking… maybe we could look at a new place. One that we both pick."

"I would love to," she grinned, and I knew I was instantly forgiven for excluding her from my plans.

It was true, though. I wanted her here forever, and I honestly couldn't have imagined my life without her at this point. She had easily and quickly become the best part of every day.

We each blissfully drifted into a deep sleep, the worries of the day before washing off of us in our postcoital high.

As the sun's rays began to creep in the room lightly, a beam of light cast on Erin's face. Even asleep, she was stunningly beautiful. Her lips parted slightly, and I could hear her breath as she looked relaxed for the first time since we reconnected.

I didn't want to slip away just yet.

Instead, I made her a hearty breakfast. The smell of crispy sausages and toasted bread filled the room as I stirred the eggs.

"That's making my mouth water…" Erin groaned sleepily.

She had since changed into a silk nightgown, which left little to the imagination.

"That makes two of us," I said as I eyed the curves of her body.

"Down, boy." Erin swatted my behind. "Is there anything I can do?" She offered, smiling.

"No, you sit. My orders."

"Bossy one, he is."

"You bet your ass I am."

Erin conceded rather quickly and retreated to the couch, where she opted for some Netflix under one of our extra-large Sherpa blankets.

When breakfast was finished, I slid the bacon out of the oven.

"Are we eating on the couch?" I called from the kitchen.

"No, I'm coming." Erin stood up, then gripped the couch for support.

Her face went pale, her eyes rolled back, and she was limp, sinking to the ground in a heap.

No!

"Erin! Erin, wake up, baby," I cried.

Her eyes opened slowly, and she was rightfully confused.

"What happened?"

"You passed out. Come on, I'm taking you to the

doctor right now." Carefully pulling her to her feet, I slid my phone and wallet into my pocket.

"Wait, let me get changed," she gestured to her nightgown.

Shit, that's right. I don't want any guy in town ogling her looking like that.

"Here, sit. I'll grab you some pajamas." I planted her on the armchair.

The wind blew Erin's hair back as she gazed out the window quietly. Other than a few protests, she hadn't said a word since we got her in the car. Apparently, passing out didn't constitute a doctor's visit, and she had "just received a clean bill of health."

You have also been through a physical ordeal.

"Hi, do you have an appointment?" A bright-eyed older receptionist with way too much lipstick on smiled.

"No, but she was here yesterday. She passed out, and she needs to be seen now."

"Sorry, sir. Without an appointment—" she began to explain.

"She needs to be seen, NOW!" My fist slammed on the counter, and I was instantly snapped back to reality.

The receptionist, Erin, and everyone in the waiting room had stopped and stared open-mouthed at the rude man yelling.

Her doctor strolled by with a stack of papers. He took in the situation quickly unfolding in front of him.

"I have a small opening. Come on back, Erin. You… you wait here." He eyed me, a glare on his face.

I know, I'm an asshole. But I can't let anything happen to her.

"If you'll just take a seat." The receptionist smiled once more, but it didn't quite reach her eyes. *Yeah, yeah, I'm sitting.*

Time moved so slowly as I waited there for her. I had asked the receptionist twice if everything was okay, but she reminded me that she could not tell me anything. Her pretend smile was fading, and it was becoming increasingly clear that I was on thin ice with her.

The waiting room cleared, refilled back up, and cleared again before they told me I was allowed to go back and see her. She looked wiped out but stunning as ever.

"How is she?" I asked the doctor, who just nodded and said she would be okay, that I could go in and see her.

Erin.

Chapter Twenty-Seven

EPILOGUE

ERIN

Exhaustion. My body had been pushed to the end of the Earth and back. I was ordered bed rest, which Damon happily obliged.

Three months later, I stood before the floor-length mirror as my mother secured my "something blue" pins into my hair.

"You are just the most beautiful bride," Cara tearfully choked out.

Lila was twirling in her flower girl dress, staring at herself in front of the mirror.

"You're going to make me cry," I warned.

My mother sighed softly behind me, letting me know she was done.

"I'm ready?" I checked.

"You, my dear, are ready. Damon won't know what hit him," my mom winked at me.

Cara grabbed her bouquet, readying Lila as they lined

up at the door. Music started to flow, and one by one, they exited.

"That's your cue," my dad said as he appeared at my side, linking my arm with his.

His support wasn't always there initially, but after Jonas took me, he proved himself one of our biggest supporters.

"Don't let me fall."

"Never." He pushed the double doors open, and I could see Damon standing in the distance. The aisles were packed with our friends from town and our close family. A smile spread across my husband-to-be's face as I made my way to him.

My heart thundered in my chest, excitement and anticipation battling against one another.

As my father gave me away, I could see tears brimming in his eyes.

Don't cry, Dad.

"Hi," Damon whispered, taking my hand.

"Hi."

"Dearly beloved, we are gathered here today to…" the officiant started.

I couldn't take my eyes off Damon the entire time. His eyes drew me in, and his hands firmly held me in place, as if there was anywhere else I would rather be. He was home to me.

"I do," Damon retorted, not a moment of hesitation.

"Erin?"

"I do."

"Damon, you may now kiss your bride."

Applause erupted around us as he dipped me, his mouth covering mine as his tongue quickly entered, swirling with mine.

Not here, not yet.

"Ladies and gentlemen, I present to you the new Mr. and Mrs. Clark!"

Our hands found each other as we walked past our beaming guests and into the suite we had for the night.

The plan was to take photos for an hour while the reception guests ordered drinks and had appetizers.

"That was…" I turned to Damon, who had locked the door behind him.

"Yeah…" His hands grabbed my ass, pinning me to the wall.

My dress was big, bulky, and clearly in the way. Careful not to ruin it, he disconnected the skirt portion before lifting me onto the table.

"You looked so stunning up there, baby. All I wanted to do was taste you," his hands fingered the delicate white lace adorning my body before ripping the bottom half open.

"You're already so wet for me," he groaned before his tongue attacked me.

My hands gripped the table edges for support, but Damon used his other hand to steady me. One hand found my clit, applying the most excruciatingly wonderful pressure as I gripped his tie, pulling him closer.

"Oh god, Damon, what about the guests?" I moaned.

"Fuck the guests," a growl escaped his throat.

My husband.

He stood suddenly, flipping me over onto my stomach.

"Enough baby, I need to feel you right now."

The head of his cock pressed at my entrance, and I leaned forward, giving him full access to my pussy.

"I could never get tired of this." He thrust in, my walls squeezing tight around him.

One hand gripped my throat from behind as his other softly palmed my ass.

I clenched up at the momentary thought.

"Easy baby, we'll take this slow." Damon pulled his hand back, popping it in his mouth.

As he pumped in and out, he took his wet finger and rubbed it on my rear, pushing slowly into the entrance.

"Oh… *fuck*," I breathed.

The feeling was foreign, yet so deliciously pleasurable.

Slowly, his finger began to move in and out.

This is amazing.

"Damon, I want to try all of you," I whispered.

"Here, baby?" His finger curled.

"Yes."

He withdrew his cock from my throbbing pussy, spreading some lube on it quickly. He positioned himself at the entrance once more, and I swallowed in anticipation.

Very carefully, I took all of him until I was full with him. Damon was gentle, slowly starting to move.

This is exquisite.

"Are you okay, baby?"

"Yes, don't stop."

"This feels fucking amazing," he grunted, his hand slapping my ass hard.

He started to move then, each more intense than the last. I felt my orgasm quickening.

"I'm there, baby," I cried, gripping the edge tighter.

"Fuck, Erin," he spilled into me as my walls tightened, losing control around him.

"That was…"

"Wow," he agreed.

I cleaned myself up, resecured my dress, and then sat on the couch to collect myself. My husband joined me.

"Who knew?" He winked at me.

We had been talking about trying anal for weeks, and I knew I was going to surprise him with it on our wedding day. I just figured it would be at night when all the guests had left.

"Ready to rejoin the crazies?" I laughed, taking his hand in mine.

"After you, Mrs. Clark."

The End

About the Author

Jennifer Rivers is an emerging author of contemporary romance novels with a little touch of mystery. She lives in New England with her husband, kids, and her two crazy pups.

When she's not dreaming up her next enemies to lovers or brother's best friend suspenseful romance. She spends her time out and about with her kids or in the kitchen feeding her cooking passion.

Go ahead and click "+Follow" to be notified of all upcoming releases!

Also by Jennifer Rivers

Straight Up Single Dad

Fireman's Forbidden Flame

Did you like this book? Then you'll LOVE Jennifer's other suspenseful romance The Rancher's Fake Fiancé

Sneak Peek

Lexi

The moment I stepped off the bus, the distinctive scent of Silver Creek enveloped me: a blend of fresh mountain air and the distant horses from the ranches. The general store, unchanged, still stood proudly. Its wooden facade was a silent witness to countless memories. Children's laughter drifted towards me, and, for a moment, it felt like I had never left.

"Feels good to be home," I whispered, my boots crunching the gravel beneath.

I was reaching down for my bags when a familiar voice, infused with a warmth and urgency, called out. "Lexi!"

Lifting my gaze, I found my brother barreling toward me. We met in a tight embrace. "I've missed you more than you know," he murmured.

Pulling away, I teased, "It's only been two years, Jake. Not a lifetime."

His eyes twinkled with mischief, though an undercurrent of

concern was evident. "Still, you've changed. College did wonders."

I grinned. "Just enough to dodge your playful banter."

Jake chuckled. As we began the journey home, I couldn't help but notice the subtle weight in his steps, his occasional glances over his shoulder, as though expecting something—or someone. "Alright, Jake," I probed, "you've got that look. What's going on?"

He hesitated, seemingly gathering his thoughts. "Remember Luke Dalton?"

At the mention of the name, a familiar shiver raced down my spine, a cocktail of memories and suppressed feelings. "Luke? Of course, how could I forget?" I replied, hoping my voice didn't betray my flood of emotion.

Jake, seemingly oblivious to my reaction, continued, "He's... different now, Lex. More intense. And it's not just him. There are new people in town. They've been snapping up properties left and right, and they're... different."

"What does Luke have to do with these newcomers?" I asked, trying to keep the conversation casual while my heart raced.

Pulling into the driveway, Jake got out and unloaded my bags. We walked inside, and the familiar feeling of home washed over me.

But before I could truly settle into the comforts of home, Jake gripped my arm, his face etched with urgency. "We need to talk, Lexi."

Taken aback, I met his gaze, seeing a depth of worry I hadn't noticed before. "Alright, what's the matter?"

He motioned me to follow him to the living room, still filled with brown leather and old books. "It's Luke's ranch," he didn't bother to sit. "It's under threat."

I frowned. "Threat? How?"

Jake paced, each step heavy with tension. "The damn local council, alongside some big-shot corporations, have taken an interest in his land. Rumors are, they're planning to turn it into a luxury resort."

My heart raced, anger boiling within me. "That's bullshit. That land has been in Luke's family for generations!"

"I know, Lex," Jake shot back, his face strained. "But here's the twist. To change the tide of opinion, to present the ranch as an integral part of the community, we've got a... plan."

Suspicion crept in. "What kind of plan?"

Jake glanced at me as if gauging my reaction in advance. "We need Luke to be... engaged."

My heart missed a beat. A barrage of memories with Luke, all hidden from the world, flashed through my mind. "Engaged? To who?"

Jake met my eyes squarely, a hint of desperation in his voice. "To you, Lexi."

I felt the blood drain from my face. "What? Are you out of your freaking mind?"

"It's just a ruse, Lex!" Jake exclaimed. "We think tying Luke to a known local, especially a Barrows, might just be the push we need. It'll strengthen the ranch's stance."

My thoughts spiraled. He had no idea about the clandestine nights, the secret meetings, the love that had grown and faltered in the shadows. "Has Luke agreed to this?" I managed to ask, trying to keep my voice steady.

Jake scratched the back of his neck, clearly uncomfortable. "He's out in Helena, getting supplies. He doesn't know yet. But we're running out of time."

I took a deep breath, trying to align my thoughts. Playing this part would mean reopening old wounds, diving deep into a past I had tried hard to bury. "Jake, this isn't a simple charade. This could change everything."

His eyes softened, the weight of his desperation evident. "I know I'm asking a lot. But it's not just the ranch at stake. It's our history, our community."

I sighed. "Okay. I'm not saying yes. But I am saying I'm hungry. Can we talk more over dinner?"

Click Here to keep reading

Printed in Great Britain
by Amazon